THE
SINNER'S
SON

AIMEE NICOLE WALKER

THE
SINNER'S
SON

CHAPTER ONE

THE RAPID *WHOOSH WHOOSH WHOOSH* OF THEIR BABY'S heartbeat filled the exam room, and Sawyer's pulse raced to catch up and synchronize with it. He released the breath he'd been holding and squeezed Royce's hand. The grainy white image on the black screen blurred as tears filled his eyes. *Their baby.* Blinking the moisture away, Sawyer brought their tiny miracle into focus once more. "She's gotten so much bigger," he said.

"Or he," Lucy cautioned. The ultrasound technician rocked a bubble-gum-pink pixie hairstyle that conjured thoughts of fairy dust and magic. "The sex organs are present, but it's too early for me to see them at thirteen weeks."

"Girl," Sawyer, Royce, and Kelsey declared at once. The trio looked at each other and laughed.

"We just know," Sawyer explained.

Lucy surrendered with one hand since the other was busy scanning Kelsey's stomach. "But, yes, Baby Locke has grown a lot. She was about the size of a kidney bean during your eight-week scan, and now she's the size of a plum or a lime."

"Our Lil Plum," Royce said, his voice thick with awe.

The grainy white image bounced on the screen, and Sawyer sucked in a sharp breath. "What was that? Is she okay?"

Kelsey giggled and reached for Sawyer's other hand. "She's just a very active Lil Plum. Right, Lucy?"

"Yes, and that's what we want to see."

"Can you feel her move, Kels?" Sawyer asked.

"Not yet, but I should experience a light fluttering soon, like butterflies flitting about in there. The bigger she gets, the more pronounced her movements become."

"I can't wait to feel her kicks from the outside," Sawyer said.

Kelsey squeezed his hand. "Just a few more months."

"Women's bodies are freaking amazing," Royce added. "What a miracle."

"Yes, we are," Kelsey replied smugly. Lucy paused the scan long enough to bump fists with her.

They watched as their perfect angel bounced around like she was trying to avoid the ultrasound transducer.

Sawyer bumped his shoulder against Royce's. "Obstinate like her dad."

"I warned you," Royce said dryly.

Lucy tapped a few keys with her free hand and changed the view on the screen. "There's her heart." Lucy zoomed in a little more, and they watched the tiny chambers pulse in time with the *whooshes* filling the room. "Nice and strong at one hundred and fifty-five beats per minute."

Royce leaned into Sawyer and whispered, "This is much better than Disney World."

Tears threatened again, but this time, Sawyer didn't fight them back. "The absolute happiest time of my life."

Royce stayed remarkably dry-eyed throughout the scan until Lucy handed him an updated sonogram printout. He held it between them so they could both stare at the photo together. Royce tilted his head to rest against Sawyer's and said, "Look at our Lil Plum."

"She's perfect."

"Aw," Lucy said. "This is such a beautiful moment."

"Good thing I captured it," Kelsey said. "This photo would be great for the first page of her baby book."

Sawyer looked up just as she set her phone on the exam table. "Thank you. I was too busy experiencing the moment to even think about documenting it."

"I'm going to show this to Bones and Dolly when we get home, and then I'm going to hang it up on the refrigerator," Royce announced proudly.

Sawyer forced his gaze away from Lil Plum's image. "We better wait until after we announce the pregnancy to our family and coworkers."

Royce grimaced. "Yeah. Stumbling across the sonogram picture isn't the way I want anyone to find out, especially Evangeline."

Lucy wiped the gel off Kelsey's stomach and pushed her cart to the corner of the room. "Dr. Yang will be in shortly. She's running slightly behind after an emergency C-section early this morning."

"Thanks, Lucy," the trio called out.

"You're welcome. See you all at your next scan."

Silence fell over the room, but the *whoosh whoosh whoosh* still played in Sawyer's mind. He closed his eyes to hold on to the memory longer. He'd fallen in love with the sound at the eight-week scan and wished he could hear it all the time. Lil Plum's heartbeat got louder, and Sawyer opened his eyes to find Kelsey smiling at him. She held up her phone to show that she'd recorded a portion of the ultrasound.

"They'll record the heartbeat onto a tiny device for you at our twenty-week scan, and you can tuck it inside a stuffed animal," Kelsey said. "They have plushies to go with nearly every nursery theme. You'll be able to hear Lil Plum's heartbeat whenever you want. We put Ella's recording inside the cutest little Highland cow and used it in our pregnancy announcement."

Royce wrapped his arm around Sawyer's shoulders and kissed his temple. "I can't wait to share our big news."

"Me too," Sawyer said. "But when and how?"

"Our families are gathering at your parents' house in two weeks for Labor Day," Royce replied. "We can pull our parents aside for a private reveal and then do something else to announce the news to our extended family and friends gathered there."

"Pinterest will have tons of fun ideas to look at," Kelsey said. "Oh! We'll need to come up with something to announce it at work."

Royce's eyes danced with mischief as he rubbed his hands together. "I'm looking forward to that."

Sawyer got the feeling their pregnancy announcement would end up resembling a prank. He groaned and massaged his temple. "Let's just keep that one simple. A nice cake shaped like a onesie that announces our due date or something. And we should probably tell Mendoza and HR immediately."

"Or—"

A knock on the door interrupted whatever Royce had been about to say. With any luck, he'd forget all about the idea when it came time to plan the announcement. Dr. Naomi Yang entered the exam room with a pleasant smile on her face and an ornery gleam in her eyes. Sawyer had liked the ob-gyn from the moment they'd met, and he understood why Kelsey had chosen her. Dr. Yang's qualifications alone were impressive, but it was her charismatic bedside manner that he liked most.

Dr. Yang made eye contact with each of them before asking, "How are we doing?"

"I feel great," Kelsey said.

"Great," Sawyer and Royce chorused.

"That's wonderful to hear." Dr. Yang sat down, opened her laptop, and began typing. "How's your nausea, Kelsey?"

"Not bad at all," she replied. "Brushing my teeth is the worst part, but I'm usually in fighting form after that. I get an occasional bout in the afternoon, but it's nothing my ginger lollipops or teas can't cure."

"That's good. Are you sleeping well?" Dr. Yang asked.

"Ten hours every night," Kelsey said. "I wish I could sleep like this all the time."

They went through a series of routine questions about nutrition and hydration before Dr. Yang turned her attention to them. "Do you have questions for me, dads?" She'd clocked Sawyer as a nervous Ned during their first appointment, but she'd seemed charmed instead of annoyed by his list of prepared questions.

"Not this time." Sawyer looked at Royce, who shook his head.

"All right. Let me know if that changes." Dr. Yang stood up and approached the table to do a physical exam. She gently pressed Kelsey's abdomen and measured her uterus before returning to her laptop to enter the data. She clicked around to review the images from the ultrasound and Kelsey's urine test results from the lab. "Everything looks great with the baby and Kelsey," Dr. Yang said. "Keep up the great work. Drink tons of water to stay hydrated during these scorching August temperatures."

"Will do," Kelsey said as she sat up and adjusted her shirt.

"See you all in four weeks."

Once they were alone, Royce turned to Kelsey. "Where do you want to eat for lunch?"

Kelsey lowered her head and angled it to the side as if listening to her belly. She straightened back up and said, "Lil Plum says Mexican."

"Are you going to play this cool?" Royce asked when they arrived back at the precinct after lunch. He parked the SUV in the lot but left the engine running. "You're literally vibrating with excitement."

"I don't know," Sawyer admitted. "I haven't tried to keep a secret this big since coming out as gay. Ro, I've never been this happy before, and I don't know how to process this surge of emotions. My heart can't possibly expand further without exploding." He placed a hand over his chest, hoping the steady rise and fall of his lungs would help center him. All he felt was the continued swelling of gratitude, love, and joy. "I'm a human can of biscuits on the verge of bursting at the seams."

"That's just a buildup of gases from the heavy lunch we consumed," Royce said, patting his stomach.

Denial danced on the tip of Sawyer's tongue, but his lips wouldn't form the lie. "The three of us devoured a basket and a half of chips and probably a half gallon of queso before they brought our food out."

"And then I shoveled the rice and beans into my mouth like it was my last meal," Royce said. "I need to finish setting up for the open house tonight, but all I want is a Gas-X pill and a nap."

Sawyer snorted, and it must've acted as a valve release because the pressure in his chest eased slightly. "Can't believe you're comparing our baby joy to indigestion and heartburn."

Royce unbuckled his seat belt and leaned across the console. "Two things can be true at the same time."

Sawyer freed himself also and met his husband halfway, cupping Royce's face. "*You* make me incredibly happy. You're the reason for my surging joy and the overstuffed feeling, not because I ate too much for lunch."

Waggling his brows, Royce pressed his lips to Sawyer's. "Stuffing you is my favorite thing to do."

Sawyer groaned and lowered his head to Royce's shoulder.

"What?" Royce cupped Sawyer's neck and kissed his temple. "You set me up with your phrasing. Overstuffed? You lobbed that right over home plate and expected me to swing and miss? No way."

Sawyer tilted his head back and looked to the heavens for help through the moon roof.

Royce laughed and pulled him into a tight hug that turned into a tender kiss. "Never change," Sawyer said. "Not a single damn thing about yourself."

"Because I make you happy?" Royce asked.

"The happiest."

Royce gripped Sawyer's tie to keep him in place. "And I stuff you like no one else ever has or ever will?"

Sawyer tilted his head to the side as if scrolling through memories of past lovers or considering future ones, until Royce growled his disapproval. "You're the stuff my dreams are made of, and I wouldn't trade you for anyone—past, present, or future. I love you, Ro. Having a baby with you just amplifies that emotion a thousand times. If I nearly stroke out from hearing her little heartbeat, what will it be like when we hold her for the first time? I might expire on the spot."

Royce chuckled warmly and stroked his knuckles over Sawyer's cheek. "You won't. God, our Lil Plum is so lucky to have two dads who adore her so much already." He pulled back and groaned as if just realizing something. "She's going to spend her entire life trying to escape our suffocating affection."

Sawyer barked out a laugh and flopped back in his seat. "Do you know what's worse than a helicopter mom?"

Royce pursed his lips and exhaled. "No, but I bet you're going to tell me."

"Detective dads," Sawyer said, then added, "Two of them."

Royce pointed to Sawyer and to himself. "One. Two. I can do simple math."

Sawyer playfully shoved his shoulder. "She's going to leave for college and never come back."

"We'll be lucky if she doesn't board a Greyhound bus when she's fifteen," Royce countered. "Or pull a Fred Flintstone and beat it out of here in her Little Tikes car with her chubby toddler feet. Do you know they make a pink princess cozy coupe? I damn near bought it last week."

Sawyer placed a hand on his stomach. "I think I have indigestion for real now."

"Christ, when did we become such joy killers?" Royce asked.

"When we discovered we were having Lil Plum. We're so excited that it terrifies us."

Royce looked at him with a crooked smile. "Are we going to change her nickname to a new fruit after every doctor's visit?"

Sawyer shrugged. "Maybe."

"What size will she be at sixteen weeks?" Royce asked.

"Avocado."

Royce laughed. "Yeah, she's getting a new nickname each month."

"Pumpkin is the last fruit, and I might call her that for the rest of my life."

"Awww." Royce reached for his hand. "Maybe we shouldn't fret about her trying to escape us before she's drawn her first breath."

"Agreed. We're going to have an amazing support system to help guide us when we get too overprotective," Sawyer said.

"Kels will smack some sense into us for sure." Royce pressed a quick kiss against Sawyer's lips. "No one has spotted us, so it's not too late to sneak home and play hooky." Something must've caught Royce's attention because he looked out the windshield and groaned. "Your oversized golden retriever is headed our way."

Sawyer turned to find Detective Topher Carnegie advancing toward their SUV with a purposeful stride. Royce had given the younger detective the nickname because of his tawny coloring and his charming personality traits that aligned with the popular dog breed. Royce had meant the moniker as a compliment, but Sawyer doubted Topher would like the comparison. He opened the door and stepped out of the vehicle before the cold case detective could reach him. "What's up, Toph?"

"Hey. I'm just on my way out to meet Julian for lunch. Thought I'd warn you that Alec Bishop is blowing up the precinct's phones looking for you."

Sawyer bit back a groan as his good mood shriveled up and died. "Just great," he said, though his acerbic tone implied the news was anything but.

And to think, Sawyer had been just another one of Alec's true-crime fanboys a few short months ago when they'd met at a crime convention in Denver. He'd been intrigued by the story of a man who'd discovered his estranged father was a serial killer and turned him into the FBI. Sawyer had been excited to meet Alec and was flattered when the media's latest darling was familiar with his solved cold cases. Then came the stunning news that Alec believed his father, Andrew Bishop, killed more women than the FBI had credited to him.

Alec had laid out sound logic and shown admirable determination to bring closure to those families. He wanted police departments around the country to partner with him to solve the cases, starting with

Sawyer and the SPD since his family had lived in Savannah between 1995 and 1997. Deciding to capitalize on his notoriety, Alec secured significant financial backing to fund the investigations. Everything had seemed too good to pass up, which was why Commissioner Rigby overruled all of Mendoza's concerns and paved the way for their partnership.

And that's when Alec's energy had drastically shifted from determined to obnoxious. The message-bombing was just the latest reason Sawyer regretted the decision to take part in Alec's investigative podcast. He'd been smart not to share his cell phone number with the man, but he was running out of reasons to withhold it since their partnership would begin in earnest the following week. Sawyer could already see he'd need to set hard boundaries and enforce them diligently.

"This guy is going to be a problem," Royce said as he rounded the hood and joined their conversation.

"Not for long," Sawyer promised.

His cold case squad had dedicated a lot of time and effort to getting much of the legwork done before Alec arrived. They'd successfully eliminated two out of the five potential victims just by retesting evidence against Andrew's DNA. While those cases remained unsolved, they knew Andrew wasn't their killer and had viable results to test against future suspects. Alec had come in clutch with the funding as soon as the principal participants inked the contracts.

"Gotta run," Topher said. "I don't want to keep Julian waiting."

"I'll let you know what I learn from Alec," Sawyer told him.

Topher pivoted to walk backward. "Hopefully that he's changed his mind. Julian is already angling for an introduction. I thought we'd be married longer than a year before he got bored with me."

"Ha! Julian is mad about you," Royce told him. "That creepy dude is no threat to you."

"Thanks, Ro."

"*Creepy dude?*" Sawyer asked once Topher had turned back around and disappeared into the parking lot.

"I just don't like that Bishop guy. He gets my hackles up."

Sawyer angled his head and studied Royce. "Is this going to be a problem for us?"

"No. My husband is crazy about me."

"Hell yes, he is." Sawyer squared his shoulders and faced the building. "I better go see what Alec is fired up about now."

Both the CCU and the Explorer Academy were in the basement, so they headed down together.

"See you at the open house tonight," Royce said once they stepped off the elevator.

"I can't wait to meet your new cadets."

The CCU bullpen was empty when Sawyer entered the room, and he thanked his lucky stars for a few quiet moments to transition from an ecstatic, expecting dad to an analytical detective. But of course, his desk phone rang before his ass landed in his chair. The sound felt intrusive and downright ominous, which made Sawyer scoff and shake his head. Personification worked great in fictional literature, but that kind of thinking didn't work well in police work. Phrases like whispering winds pulled Sawyer into a story and made him feel part of the scene, but he sure as hell wouldn't use that terminology in a police report. It wasn't the middle of the night, so why was he assigning negative emotions to a ringing phone? Because Sawyer had learned Alec Bishop was looking for him.

He mentally braced himself and answered the call. "This is Detective Key." But by this time, the call had already rolled over to his voicemail. Sawyer set the receiver in the cradle and wiggled his mouse to wake his computer. He'd give the caller a minute to leave a message before retrieving it. He had several emails in his inbox and even more messages in the department's instant-messaging system. Sawyer quickly scanned them and realized Topher had not exaggerated Alec's persistence. He leaned back in his chair, scrubbed a hand over his face, and resisted the urge to shout "Fuck!"

Sawyer stretched his neck muscles as if he were about to go a few rounds with a prizefighter and cycled through a cleansing breath. Most of his emails and IMs instructed him to call Alec, though they varied widely in tone and urgency. Then Sawyer moved to his voicemail inbox and played back the five messages, deleting the four from Alec and listening intently to the most recent one, which came from his forensic lab contact.

"Hi, Sawyer, it's Mia Thomas with Mayfield Forensic Services in Atlanta." Sawyer hadn't needed her full introduction since it seemed like he talked to Mia more than his own family lately. "I have the results on the evidence we tested for Joyce Cole. We found a male DNA profile, but it does not match Andrew Bishop or anyone in CODIS either. I'm zero for three and feel like I've really let you down. Hopefully, our work here at the lab will eventually help you close those cases. I will email the documentation to you soon. Please call me if you have questions. Good luck with your investigations."

Sawyer pushed back from his desk and walked over to the conference area they'd dubbed the war room. They'd set up a whiteboard for each of Andrew's potential victims. They'd started with five women: Gwen Cobb, Monica Horton, Joyce Cole, Jane Doe 1, and Jane Doe 2. After a thorough review of evidence, they determined that only three women had items that could yield DNA results for testing. The other two women had been missing for substantially longer times before their discovery and were victims of environmental degradation just as much as the monsters who'd claimed their lives. Mayfield's lab had eliminated Gwen Cob, Joyce Cole, and Jane Doe 2 as Andrew Bishop's victims. Sawyer documented the lab's finding on Joyce's whiteboard and moved it off to the side with the other two, leaving Monica and Jane Doe 1 front and center in the room. He wasn't giving up on Gwen, Joyce, or Jane Doe 2. Not by a long shot. His team would do everything in their power to get justice for them, but Alec was coming next week to focus on the two women who could be his father's victims.

He stared at the boards for a long while, noting the disparity of information between the remaining women. With Monica, knowing her identity gave them a solid starting point for an investigation. They would hopefully track down relatives or former friends who could tell them what was going on in her life at the time she went missing. They only knew the most basic information about Jane. Her approximate height and weight wouldn't yield anything, and knowing she'd once broken her tibia would only get them so far. Without her name, they couldn't get medical records for comparison. There was no starting point because none of the evidence left behind pointed them in a specific direction. Hell, their basic information for the first Jane Doe hadn't matched to any missing person report taken nationally during that timeframe. The same was true with the second Jane Doe, but at least her DNA was now in the system, and they could hopefully identify her someday.

Sawyer had been a cop for nearly fifteen years and had seen many troubling things, but the Jane and John Does hit him hardest. Was no one looking for them? That was something he couldn't accept. Sawyer knew that law enforcement was often a major part of the problem by refusing to take missing person reports for adults, as these Jane Does were. "Everyone needs to do better," he said.

His cell phone rang, and he absently answered it without checking the caller ID. "Detective Sergeant Key."

"Finally." Alec Bishop's frustrated voice snapped Sawyer back to reality. "I've been calling for hours."

"Oh, I know you have. You've created quite the stir with your unprofessional behavior."

"I didn't mean to," Alec said.

"Of course you did. Why else would you have done it?"

"I was excited to talk to you about our project, but you didn't return my calls." Alec sounded like a spoiled child instead of the investigator he wanted to be.

Sawyer pinched the bridge of his nose. "If you must know, I've been out of the office on personal business."

"Oh." Alec's irritation deflated like a balloon. "Is everything okay?"

"Yes," Sawyer replied simply. "How did you get my cell phone number?"

Alec snorted. "Are you joking? What kind of investigator can't ferret out someone's phone number?"

"I'm not just someone," Sawyer reminded him. "I'm a police detective."

"And your information is just as vulnerable as anyone else's if you know how to look for it."

A fact that made Sawyer's blood run cold. "Do I need to remind you that I'm the real investigator in this partnership?"

"Seems like you just did," Alec snapped.

Sawyer gripped the phone tighter and fought the urge to tell Alec Bishop to go fuck himself. He trained his gaze on Monica's and Jane's whiteboards. There was hope for these women, and Sawyer didn't want to let them down. So, he let the smart-ass comeback go. "I received a call from the lab, and they excluded your father as the assailant in another case."

"Damn," Alec said. "Another swing and a miss."

"At least it helps us focus our resources on the final two."

"And one's a Jane Doe, right?" Alec asked.

"Yes." Sawyer gritted his teeth and braced himself for a shitty remark.

"I really hope you find resolutions in all these cases, but especially the Janes. I wouldn't wish that on anyone." Even a broken clock was right twice a day. "And you're not the only one with news."

"Yeah? What's up?"

"I'll be in Savannah sooner than I'd planned."

Sawyer barely managed to bite back a groan. Alec wasn't supposed to arrive until Sunday, and he'd planned to make the most of his final days of freedom. "When?"

"In two hours."

Sawyer's heart sank. "That's soon."

"The house I'm renting on Tybee Island opened up sooner than expected. I guess the previous renter had to end their vacation early. The homeowner reached out to see if I wanted to take advantage of the vacancy for a discounted price. Couldn't pass up that offer."

"Of course not." Could his voice sound drier or more brittle?

"Let's get dinner tonight and kick around some ideas. The rest of my crew won't arrive until Sunday, but we can get a jump start on the project."

"I'm sorry, but I can't."

"No to just dinner or..."

"All of it," Sawyer said. "My husband has an open house for his Explorer cadets to kick off the new school year starting next week. I have other investigations that require my attention right now, and some of them are on the verge of breakthroughs."

Alec was quiet for so long that Sawyer wondered if their call had dropped. But then he blew out a frustrated breath. "You can't just shuffle things around for me?" This attitude was the reason Sawyer needed to set boundaries and enforce them.

"No, I cannot. I've already moved my schedule around to accommodate you, and you agreed to the terms. You and I have plans to meet Monday morning at eight thirty, and I'm going to stick to that."

"That's disappointing," Alec said.

With anyone else, Sawyer would've apologized for letting them down, but that would give Alec an opening he'd exploit at every opportunity. "Do you need recommendations for things to do in town since you're arriving early?"

Alec laughed humorlessly. "Nah. I tracked down your phone number, so I can probably find something to entertain me for the next four days."

"Sounds good. See you Monday morning at eight thirty." Sawyer disconnected the call before Alec could get another word in. Then he turned his full attention back to the whiteboards. Would they be able to tie Andrew Bishop to Monica or Jane?

"Hey, Sawyer," Holly said from the conference room doorway.

He turned to greet her. "Hey, Holls. What's up?"

"That tiny break in my aggravated armed robbery investigation has turned into a major fissure. Judge Stanley signed off on my arrest warrants."

"Congratulations."

"Thanks," Holly said. "There'd been no movement for several years on this case, and then BAM! People finally started talking about what they knew. This case has grown into something much bigger than I expected. I have four arrests to make, and these aren't good dudes. All of them have lengthy records and have served time in jail."

"And it's doubtful they want to return," Sawyer said.

"Exactly. I want to coordinate with Sergeant Reynolds for tactical support. I need to hit this crew with simultaneous takedowns at the ass crack of dawn to avoid them tipping each other off." Holly wasn't there to seek his permission or his approval. She knew damn well she already had those. What Holly needed from him was a signature to request precious resources from an ever-shrinking budget.

"Let's do this."

CHAPTER TWO

"So, we meet again," Sawyer said.

Kelsey snickered from his right side. "Feels like déjà vu. Like maybe we just did this a few hours ago."

"The chairs at the doctor's office were more comfortable," Royce whispered from Sawyer's left. "And this feels more like a visit to the principal's office. Dr. Yang has way more chill than our chief."

Maeve stepped out of Mendoza's office and smiled at them before reclaiming her seat behind her pristine desk. The personal assistant's good-natured expression did not fool Sawyer for one second. She opened a drawer and pulled a cookie tin from its depths and set it on the desk. "Chief Mendoza isn't his usual jovial self, so take this with you. I'm sure his mood is nothing an afternoon cookie and a cup of coffee can't cure. He has the latter already, so my peanut butter cookies should tip the scale in your favor."

Royce snorted. "Jovial?" Leave it to him to voice the private thoughts out loud.

The fair-haired assistant sat up straighter in her chair and looked affronted by the question. Maeve obviously got to see a side of the chief they didn't. Mendoza was the fairest man Sawyer had ever met, and he was certain their chief held his officers in the highest regard, but none of them would ever describe the man as jovial. Mendoza's smile was as rare as the Hope Diamond that may or may not have existed and may or may not be at the bottom of the ocean. Sawyer exchanged a glance with Kelsey. Their thoughts aligned with Royce's, but they weren't going down with the sinking ship, and if Royce wasn't careful, he'd find himself afloat without a door to cling to. He really needed to stop watching *Titanic* every time it popped up on a streaming menu.

"You don't agree?" Maeve asked casually while tucking a wavy lock behind her ear.

Sawyer sensed a trap and subtly nudged Royce with his elbow, willing his husband to use the filter in his beautiful brain, but his efforts went ignored. If her earrings came off, Royce would need to fend for himself.

"Jovial sounds like jolly," Royce said. "That makes me think of Santa Claus. I think affable works better in this situation. Wouldn't you?" He looked at Sawyer and Kelsey for support but got crickets in return.

Maeve's blue eyes twinkled with humor as she took in the trio. "Uh-huh." Her desk phone rang before she could comment further.

"That was close," Kelsey whispered. "Keep it up and there won't be room for you on the door." She started humming "My Heart Will Go On" by Celine Dion.

Sawyer laughed. "I had the same thought." He turned to Royce. "But notice we didn't voice them."

Royce rolled his eyes at their shenanigans. "Are you nervous about the conversation with Mendoza?"

"A little." Sawyer turned and met his husband's gaze. "But I don't know if I feel like a kid waiting outside the principal's office."

Royce's gorgeous mouth curved into a smirk. "Because the Golden Boy never got in trouble."

"Until I met you," Sawyer said. Rigby had summoned them to her office more than once when she'd been their chief.

"Were you the schoolyard snitch?" Kelsey asked Sawyer.

"Hell no. My brother and sister told me what happened to them. *Stitches*," Sawyer whispered dramatically.

Royce looked around him to smile at Kelsey. "Can't you just see him writing his classmate's infractions in a notebook?"

"Absolutely," Kelsey replied.

"Your names would be at the top of my snitch list," Sawyer told them. "Beautiful people picking on the nerdy, chubby kid."

Kelsey hooked her arm through Sawyer's and leaned her head on his shoulder. "I would've kicked anyone's ass who picked on you." She pointed a lavender-tipped nail in Royce's direction. "It would've been a weekly beatdown with this one, I bet."

"Probably daily," Royce said with a sigh. "I would've been jealous of everything Sawyer had, and it would've spilled out of me in the ugliest ways. It's all I knew back then."

"But you're an amazing man now," Sawyer said. If they were alone, he would've kissed Royce, but the chief wouldn't appreciate PDA in the precinct, especially right outside his office.

A metallic clank interrupted their sweet moment, and Sawyer turned to look at Maeve. She'd removed the lid from the tin and helped herself to a cookie, watching them with a sappy expression on her face as she chewed. "I love your love." Her face turned bright pink, as if she couldn't believe she'd said that out loud. "Sorry," she squeaked.

Sawyer smiled to ease her embarrassment. "That's very sweet of you to say." The click of high heels on a tile floor caught his attention, and he turned to see who approached. His eyes widened when he saw

Audra Teller from Human Resources making a beeline for them. Her no-nonsense stride matched the serious cut of her navy pantsuit. The only vibrant color on Audra was her fiery red hair, which she'd slicked back into a bun. "The chief called HR without knowing why we requested a meeting?"

Maeve shrugged. "He must've done so after I left."

"And now I know what it feels like to visit the principal's office," Sawyer grumbled.

"He actually saved us time by inviting her to join us," Kelsey said. "Which means he knows why we want to see him."

Royce nodded sagely. "So it would seem."

Sawyer glanced at Maeve, who devoured the unfolding scene with wide, unblinking eyes, her half-eaten cookie now suspended partway to her mouth. He didn't know Maeve very well, but she wouldn't work for Mendoza if she gossiped, so he classified her reaction as natural curiosity. Their secret would be safe for the time being. If his mother found out about Kelsey carrying her grandchild through the rumor mill... Well, it didn't bear thinking about.

Audra stopped when she reached Maeve's desk and straightened her navy blazer. "I got here as soon as I could," she said, sounding slightly winded. "Mendoza said it was important. Do you know what's going on?"

Maeve shrugged before tipping her head in their direction. "No, but these are your likely culprits," she said before taking a bite of her cookie.

Audra cocked her head to the side and studied them with shrewd, dark eyes. "I expected this day with one of you," she said, her gaze lingering on Royce. "Will someone from Internal Affairs be joining us? Do any of you need union representation?"

Mendoza's door opened before they could respond. "Oh, good."

The chief's flat tone said he meant the exact opposite. "Let's do this." He turned on his heels, leaving his office door open.

Audra fixed Royce with a scowl. "What did you do?"

"*Me?* Why not them?" His mock outrage didn't move her conviction one iota.

"Get real, Locke. Do you need a union rep?"

"Hey, I'm innocent," Royce claimed.

"Well…" Kelsey said.

Sawyer immediately jumped on the bandwagon. "You are a major part of why we're here."

"I knew it," Audra groaned. "I don't know if I should run for the hills or hustle into the chief's office to put out the fires you've started." Both hands went to her hips. "Level with me. Are we talking tiny embers or a five-alarm blaze?"

"You'll find out faster if everyone comes inside," Mendoza called out from the depths of his office. "I'm not the one who instigated this meeting, and I have many things to accomplish today. Tick tock, you're on the clock."

Audra glowered at Royce before pivoting on her stilettos and marching into Mendoza's office with her head held high. Royce and Kelsey filed into a single line and followed her at a more leisurely pace, leaving Sawyer to bring up the rear.

Maeve, who was hanging on to every word they'd uttered, quickly replaced the lid on the tin of cookies and slid it across the desk. "Take these," she whispered. "Trust me."

Sawyer snagged the tin and entered Mendoza's office, shutting the door behind him. Kelsey and Audra occupied the only visitors' chairs, so he placed the tin on the desk and stood off to the side with Royce. Audra darted suspicious looks at Royce every few seconds until the chief cracked a smile.

"I suppose congratulations are in order," Mendoza said.

"I'm sorry?" Audra asked in confusion. "Whom are you addressing?"

"We're having a baby," Royce told her.

Audra's eyes widened. "The three of you?"

"Yes," Sawyer replied casually, even though it was obvious her thoughts were going in the wrong direction. He blamed his tiny display of orneriness on Royce's influence.

"I'm their surrogate," Kelsey explained. "Royce and Sawyer will be the baby's parents."

"Ah, of course." Heat flooded Audra's cheeks, and she dropped her gaze to her lap.

Sawyer felt a tiny bit guilty for playing along. "Our due date is mid-February."

"Maybe a Valentine's Day baby," Audra said, rebounding quickly.

"I asked for a representative from HR to join us to address any concerns the department might have about this situation or any pitfalls we need to steer clear of," Mendoza said.

Audra blinked for a few moments as she considered the situation. "There are no issues that I can think of. None of you work in the same department, nor do you report directly to each other, so there isn't a power imbalance issue. I think the only concern would be inappropriate comments someone might make to or about you." She cleared her throat. "Or misguided assumptions someone might make."

"No one in our departments would dare," Kelsey said. "My coworkers know how much I love my husband."

"And I don't think people question our commitment to one another either," Royce said, gesturing between himself and Sawyer.

"People will be curious, and they might say something out of line," Audra said. "We'll just deal with the situations as they arise."

"And I will deal with them severely," Mendoza stated. "I don't think anyone in this precinct will make a crass remark to any of you, but if so, it won't happen more than once."

"We'll obviously have to discuss maternity and paternity leave and address any shortages that could incur in your absences," Audra said. "And when it's time, I'll assist you with all the paperwork to add your little one to your health insurance policies and file the claims to receive your paternity leave benefits."

"Sweet," Royce said. "Nothing we need to do until then?"

"No, sir." Then Audra released a big sigh. "This is much better than I imagined when I saw Royce sitting outside the chief's office." She smiled at both men. "Congratulations." She reached over and squeezed Kelsey's hand before standing up. "And bless you. What a beautiful gift you're giving your friends."

They thanked Audra and basked in the good vibes until Mendoza cleared his throat, reminding them they were taking up his space and time.

"Sorry, Chief," Royce said. "We find ourselves just getting carried away."

"Becoming a father was the happiest moment in my life," Mendoza said. "Enjoy every second. The anticipation, the fear, and all the doubts. It will be worth it."

"Amen," Kelsey agreed as she stood up. "Thank you for your time, Chief."

Royce waited for her to pass by and fell in behind her. Sawyer moved to follow them, but Mendoza called out his name.

"I need a word with you first. Alone," Mendoza said when Royce stopped too. He made shooing motions until Royce and Kelsey were gone. "Close the door."

"Yes, Chief."

Mendoza crossed his arms and leaned back in his chair. "Why the hell was Alec Bishop ringing every damn line in this precinct to find you?"

Sawyer bit back a groan and flopped into an empty seat. "Because I didn't return his messages fast enough."

Mendoza's dark eyes held a menacing gleam. "You realize what a problem that creates for everyone."

"Yes, sir. And I'm very sorry. I talked to him when I returned to my office. I told him his behavior was unprofessional, and we've reached an understanding." Maybe if Sawyer repeated it often enough, he could manifest it into existence.

"I'm glad you've resolved the situation," Mendoza said.

Sawyer felt a *but* coming in three, two, one…

"But I can't help but think today's fiasco is just the tip of the iceberg. I don't like this guy, and I especially don't like him working with my police department." He held up his hands as if he thought Sawyer would protest. Spoiler alert: he wouldn't. "I know the potential for good. It just goes against my instincts. Maybe I'm too old-school sometimes."

"I hear you, Chief. I will do my best to keep Alec in line and his chaos to a minimum."

"That's all I ask." Mendoza smirked. "And keep your damn cell phone on you at all times."

"Yes, Chief." Sawyer cocked his head to the side. "How'd you know what we were going to tell you?"

Mendoza rolled his eyes and sighed. "I'm a veteran law enforcement officer skilled in the art of deduction." He cracked a smile before adding, "And the two of you make moon eyes at every baby or grandbaby who comes in here, so it was only a matter of time. When you both started floating through the precinct with stars shooting from your eyes, I knew the moment had arrived. Kelsey is a remarkable woman, but you already know that."

"I do, sir."

"You and Locke will make wonderful fathers." The compliment, though spoken gruffly, was the spirit boost Sawyer needed after the confrontation with Alec.

"Thank you."

Mendoza gestured to the door before pulling the tin of cookies closer. Sawyer recognized a dismissal when he saw one and got out of there as fast as he could. Royce was waiting for him, sitting in the same chair he'd vacated earlier. He quirked a brow, and Sawyer rolled his eyes.

"Walk with me and I'll catch you up."

There wasn't much to tell him, so they hadn't gotten far before Royce stopped suddenly and turned to face Sawyer. "What do you mean Alec called your cell phone? You didn't give him the number yet."

"I was getting to that part," Sawyer said, gesturing for them to keep walking before they drew attention to themselves. This time, Royce didn't interrupt. He said nothing, which was worse. "I'm handling it," Sawyer told him as they waited for the elevator.

Royce didn't speak until they were enclosed in the cabin. "I don't like it. Not one damn bit. Bishop's entitled behavior is obnoxious."

"I'm handling it," Sawyer repeated.

"I heard you the first time." Royce turned and leaned against the paneled wall. "You're not the problem." While his voice was softer, the storm raged on in his gray eyes. "Alec Bishop is the problem, and I can't shake the feeling that you're going to regret getting involved in his project."

"Not if it solves one of these cold cases." Sawyer's tone was sharper than he'd intended, and he felt an immediate twinge of guilt.

Royce stepped closer but didn't touch him, at least not with his hands or body. Those eyes though. They caressed every intimate part of Sawyer's soul and left him wishing they were alone. "But at what cost?"

"Alec's project has already funded nearly forty thousand dollars of DNA testing. I'd say the costs are going to be high."

Royce cocked a brow. "You know damn well I'm talking about the personal stakes. What if this backfires and blows up in your face?"

"It won't."

"You don't sound very convincing," Royce told him. "And I'm concerned about you maintaining your objectivity."

"I have things under control." Sawyer sounded defensive, which was the first clue that Royce could be right. His thoughts about the cases, especially the Jane Does, had turned personal. Seeing his Lil Plum on the ultrasound intensified his desire to make the world a better place, but he had to keep his objectivity to do that. Compartmentalizing had been the hardest skill Sawyer learned in his early days in law enforcement. It often felt cold or cruel to even want to sweep things into a box and close the lid, but it was necessary if he wanted a successful personal life and career. Sawyer exhaled slowly and relaxed his tensed jaw and shoulders. "I'll get things under control."

Royce stepped forward again, stopping a few inches away. Though their bodies still didn't touch, the warmth in Royce's gaze wrapped Sawyer in a tender embrace. "Your tenacity to get justice for the forgotten is just a small reason I love you so damn much. But every warrior needs to rest. It makes them better fighters."

Ding.

The elevator car stopped at the basement level, and the doors swished open. Neither Sawyer nor Royce made the first step to get off. When the doors started to close again, Royce held the button to keep them open. He cupped Sawyer's face and said, "Alec Bishop wants to charge in here like a hero who saves the day, but he's an agitator who stirs the shit. No one who respects you would've acted the way he did today. Keep that in mind."

"I will." Sawyer tilted his head toward the open door. "Want to finish this conversation in my office?"

By conversation, he meant a make-out session behind his closed door to chase away any lingering tension between them. Royce winked and gestured for him to exit first. Sawyer stepped off the elevator and nearly collided with Royce's co-director at the academy. Tara South was usually the epitome of calm, cool, and collected, so her mussed hair and wild-eyed expression caught Sawyer off guard.

"I was just heading to your office to see if lover boy was hiding there," Tara said.

Royce hopped off the elevator with a ta-da flourish and started singing a song from the band Lover Boy. He'd almost made it to the chorus before he took in Tara's disheveled appearance and frustrated expression. "Uh-oh. What happened?"

"Everything." Tara snapped off a list of things that had malfunctioned or gone wrong, including the appetizers they'd ordered from a caterer. "What makes them think an event for teenagers would serve artichoke and lobster dip or mini Wellington beef bites?"

Royce looked at Sawyer. "This sounds like some bougie shit you'd serve at poker night."

Sawyer snorted. "Not to teenagers. I can run to the store and buy a ton of bagel bites and buffalo popcorn chicken. You can send those caterers directly to my office."

Tara pointed at him. "You know what, I might just take you up on that offer if the caterer can't come up with a decent solution." She turned her attention to Royce. "Say goodbye to your husband. We have fires to extinguish."

Royce turned somber eyes to him. "Goodbye, husband."

Sawyer placed a hand over his heart. "Never goodbye. Only so long."

"Christ," Tara snarled as she strode away.

Royce walked backward a few steps. "Wish me luck."

"Break a leg."

"Don't threaten me with a good time," Royce said. "That sounds preferable to the current shit show."

"Everything is going to be great. You'll see."

"Your husband just jinxed us," Tara called out.

"No such thing," Royce and Sawyer said together.

"Great," Tara yelled. "A double jinx. We're fucked."

The approval for Holly's tactical support came through late in the afternoon, and planning for the future takedowns started immediately. This was the biggest operation Sawyer's department had ever conducted, and it was important that they plan for every contingency to avoid injury or loss of life. Luckily, Sergeant Reynolds was like-minded, and she recommended thorough surveillance on the suspects to make sure their strategy would work. They needed to know how and when these men moved and how many people might be in their residences when they served the warrants. Vehicle registrations, property deed searches, aerial photos, and even Google Earth images only got you so far. None of those things warned of potentially harmful exposures, unidentified threats, or if children lived at the premises. It was better to take their time and do it right. These four men had eluded charges on their crimes for years, and there was no reason for them to think their luck was about to change.

The extended operation required support to set up surveillance on the four suspects, so they expanded their team to include a few of the vice detectives Holly worked with before moving to cold cases. The reunion was enthusiastic, loud, and a little too long for Sawyer's liking. He tried not to check his watch every five minutes as the crew regaled the room with the highlights of their careers. Sawyer would've enjoyed the stories if they were grabbing a drink at Joe's, but they were in the middle of planning a mission. And Royce's open house had started fifteen minutes ago. He checked his watch and grimaced. Make that twenty. His phone pinged with an incoming text from Royce asking if he was okay. *Great.* His husband probably thought Alec Bishop had abducted him. Sawyer replied that his strategy meeting had run late, and he'd be there as soon as possible. Then he pocketed his phone and caught Holly's gaze. She must've clocked his growing frustration because she gave him a subtle nod.

Detective Shawn Ashcroft kept the reverie going with a robust "Hey, remember that one time—"

"At band camp," Holly interjected. "Sergeant Reynolds doesn't care where you've put your flute, buddy. We're interested in your other areas of expertise."

Instead of getting pissed at her joke, Ashcroft playfully puffed up his chest like Gaston from *Beauty and the Beast.* He even deepened his voice and said, "Which one? I have so many."

"Surveillance," Holly said.

Ashcroft deflated like a balloon. "That's my least favorite."

Holly patted his shoulder. "I know, but it's important. Let's finish up, and I'll buy you a beer at Joe's. You can tell me all about your flute stories."

"I don't know that reference," Ashcroft said. When Holly started to tell him about the scene from *American Pie,* he waved her off. "I don't need to know."

Sergeant Reynolds threw her head back and laughed. "Count me in for drinks at Joe's. Who else is coming?"

"I can't tonight," Sawyer said. "I'm going to the open house for Royce's Explorer cadets."

Ashcroft stiffened. "Shit. That's going on right now. Get out of here. We've got this."

Sawyer caught Holly's gaze, and she nodded. "I'll bring you up to speed first thing in the morning."

"Perfect." Sawyer turned to Sergeant Reynolds. "Thanks for your assist on this one."

"That's what I'm here for," she replied.

He excused himself and made a beeline for the community gathering space on the opposite side of the basement. The hum of combined voices grew louder as he approached, sounding like another one of Royce's events had reached full capacity. The Explorer program provided area high school students with an introduction to the wide spectrum of law enforcement careers while developing leadership skills and encouraging character development through community involvement. Enthusiasm and enrollment for Royce's program had exceeded everyone's wildest imagination, and the school had outgrown its current facility in only a few years. But Sawyer didn't see the department making expansion plans soon since the academy was still in its infancy.

He made the last turn in the corridor and saw that a large group of people had gathered outside the community center double doors. Sawyer recognized one of the faces from work, but he didn't know the others. They were too old to be cadets but too young to be their parents. Older siblings? The group leaned as one to peer into the room before quickly putting their heads together in discussion. A few of them shimmied, others giggled, and another one snapped her fingers repeatedly. What the hell was going on? Had Royce invited a guest speaker and forgotten to mention it?

Royce. Were these members of his fan club? It didn't matter that at least five of the people were older than Eddie. No age group was immune to that Locke magnetism. The idea amused Sawyer and even charmed him. But his delight turned to dread when he caught bits and pieces of the group's conversation.

Cory, a sandy-haired forensic science technician for the department, practically vibrated with excitement as he stared into the community room. "He's even sexier in person than he is on TV. I've never understood what bedroom eyes meant until now." Turning his attention back to the group, Cory closed his eyes and swayed. "I've never seen that shade of green. They look like sea glass. And his dark, tousled hair..."

Sawyer knew damn well who Cory was talking about since the technician had cornered him at the precinct after he'd returned from the crime convention in Denver. Cory had gushed about Alec's good looks and intelligence for an uncomfortably long stretch of time before Sawyer could free himself from the conversation. But Alec couldn't be the reason for Cory's current euphoric state, right? Because Sawyer had specifically told the pain in the ass that he'd see him on Monday morning at eight thirty.

"I can't believe you didn't tell us Alec was coming to Savannah," a gray-haired lady said to Cory. "We had to find out about his special project with your police department when he went live on Instagram."

"I didn't know anything about it, Dodie," Cory claimed, his honey-brown eyes flashing with excitement. "What special project? Did he give specifics?"

"You need to introduce yourself to him," a woman in her early twenties suggested before anyone answered his question.

"No way," Cory said. "What would I say?"

"Tell him about your specialty and offer to help with his project," Dodie replied.

Cory shook his head vigorously. "No way."

Fuck. Me. The urge to turn around and walk the other way grabbed Sawyer by the balls, but he continued to the community room, skirting around Alec's fan club as he went. Christ. Sawyer knew Alec had a large following, but he hadn't expected a portion of his fan base to show up at the precinct. *Shit!* Mendoza would be furious and blame Sawyer for all of it. At least Cory was too occupied with the groupies to notice him. His relief was short-lived as soon as he stepped inside the crowded community center. Royce and Mendoza stood at one end of the room, their rigid postures and carefully blank expressions confirming Sawyer's worst fears. He followed their gazes and, even knowing what he'd see, still cringed at the sight of the cadets and their families swarmed around Alec, peppering him with questions. To make matters worse, Commissioner Rigby stood beside him and appeared to be thrilled with the excitement he generated.

Sawyer felt sick to his stomach. The open house was Tara's and Royce's time to get to know the cadets and their families, but Alec had swooped in and hijacked their evening. Where had Tara gone? A hand landed on Sawyer's shoulder and nearly scared the piss out of him. He spun around to find Tara standing behind him. "There you are. How'd it go with the caterer?"

Tara ignored his question and narrowed her eyes. "Is this your doing?" Her voice was dark and menacing, maybe an octave above a growl.

"Nope. I didn't invite Alec. I told him to be here on Monday morning." Sawyer sounded as defensive as he felt. "I'm so damn sorry, Tara."

She squeezed his shoulder again, but it was softer this time.

Probably out of pity. "Mendoza's been asking for you, so best of luck with that."

Son of a bitch. "Want to walk over with me?"

Tara snorted. "No freaking way. I'll check on the food that no one is eating. We might as well have kept the bougie bullshit food."

Seizing on the delay tactic, Sawyer followed Tara over to a long table and loaded his plate with sliders, ham-and-cheese puff pastry pinwheels, buffalo popcorn chicken, and a fried mozzarella cheese stick.

"Since when do you eat this kind of food?" Tara pointed to the platters of fresh fruits and vegetables on the opposite side of the table. "Isn't that more your type of thing?"

Sawyer shrugged and added another slider to his plate out of spite. Stress often triggered the negative eating habits that had caused him to be overweight during a huge part of his adolescence. Sawyer stared down at his plate while battling other unhealthy reactions, like guilt and shame. He'd already eaten a huge lunch and didn't want to think about the number of calories he'd consumed. Fatty finger foods were the last thing he needed, and he'd regret eating them later. His mind went into a spiral of what to do with his plate. He couldn't throw it away without looking like a dick, but he couldn't put the food back on the platters after touching it. He'd have to eat it, but then he'd feel awful later—physically and emotionally. "I, uh—"

Royce suddenly appeared by his side and took the plate from his hands. "I'm starving. Thanks." Tension pinched Royce's features, but his gaze softened when it landed on Sawyer. "Make yourself a plate."

Sawyer glanced over his shoulder and noted that Mendoza was nowhere in sight. "Where'd the chief go?"

"As far away from here as he could get, I suspect." Royce leaned into Sawyer's personal space and lowered his voice. "He told me I had to deal with you, and I shall."

Sawyer recalled the vibrating butt plug Royce used for his last punishment and had to fight off a shiver.

"Gross," Tara said. "I'm out of here."

"Hey!" Royce called out. "You can't leave me here all alone."

Tara pivoted and held up both hands with her palms out. "I'm not leaving the building, just the conversation."

Royce cackled and turned back to the table to pile on more sandwiches and cheese sticks. He glanced up and caught Sawyer watching him. "What? I'm eating for two."

Sawyer's laughter broke the anxiety gripping his chest. "God, I love you." Movement in his periphery caught his attention, and he turned to see Cory and his cohorts enter the community room. Instead of joining the conversation, they hovered around the perimeter of the group.

"What the hell is that about?" Royce asked, gesturing to the newcomers with his half-eaten slider.

Sawyer tried not to wince but failed. "The Alec Bishop Fan Club."

Royce set his sandwich on the plate. "I've lost my appetite."

Glancing at Alec again, Sawyer said, "That makes two of us."

"What's he even doing here?" Royce asked. "How'd he even know about this event?"

"This whole thing is my fault."

"Yeah," Royce said. "It kinda is. You just had to make nice with him in Denver. Still doesn't explain what he's doing here tonight though."

"I'd mentioned the open house as the reason I couldn't meet him tonight. And then I told him I had too much going on to meet with him before Monday morning."

"Uh-huh."

"And you see how well that worked out for me," Sawyer said. "There's tenacious, and then there's this guy." Sawyer was already in over his head, and the joint project had barely gotten underway.

Royce emitted a low growl. "I don't want him interfering with our lives. I don't want him showing up places he doesn't belong." Royce's growing frustration was palpable, and Sawyer wished they were alone so he could assure him with more than words.

"I don't want those things either. I'll try being more assertive with Alec." He'd handled dangerous criminals easier than this wannabe investigative podcaster.

"Guys like him don't respond to authority and assertiveness," Royce said. "You draw a line, and he will cross it. You draw boundaries, and he will crash them. Start thinking outside the box before this guy tramples your career." Royce leaned into his space. "You're a Locke now, so start thinking like one."

Sawyer smiled despite the tense situation. "I am, and I will."

He had so much more to say, but it would need to wait because one of the male cadets broke free from the pack and strode toward them. The kid was on the shorter side, slender, and moved as if the weight of the world rested on his narrow shoulders. He had black hair, fair skin, and light blue eyes. The cadet stopped abruptly a few feet away from them, as if he'd just registered their presence. He darted an uncertain glance between them, so Sawyer waved him over and maneuvered Royce out of the way.

"This is Cayden Sutton," Royce said. "Cay, this is my husband, Sawyer."

"It's good to meet you," Cayden said with a short nod.

"It's good to meet you too."

Cayden grabbed a paper plate and glanced over his shoulder at the group surrounding Alec. "Why's everyone got a boner for that guy? He's a douche."

Royce's brow furrowed in disapproval, but his eyes radiated pride that his cadet saw through Alec's veneer. Sawyer had to bite his bottom lip to keep from laughing. "Though I can't fault your assessment of Mr. Bishop, I must insist you use more appropriate language inside the facilities or while wearing your cadet uniform."

Cayden's cheeks turned pink, and he lowered his head. "Sorry about that."

Sawyer leaned toward him and lowered his voice. "But you're not wrong, my dude."

"Says the man responsible for Alec being here," Royce said. "You should've said no."

Sawyer choked down a frustrated growl and bit hard into a naked carrot stick.

"No ranch?" Cayden asked, sounding more upset by the missing condiment than by Alec crashing their open house.

"He likes kale too," Royce said in mock horror. "And not just blitzed and blended with fruits and yogurts. He eats it raw in salads and stuff."

Cayden looked pityingly at Sawyer and added another slider onto his plate. "Dude."

Sawyer shrugged and picked up a celery stick. "I like what I like."

"Celery is for decorating a plate of chicken wings," the cadet declared.

Royce fist pumped the air dramatically. "You show promising leadership, Cay."

A young man hurried through the community center doors, halted, and searched the room until his gaze landed on Cayden. A look of relief washed over his face as he started in their direction. The guy had strikingly similar features to Cayden and was obviously an older brother.

"Dane!" Cayden's entire demeanor changed when he saw him. His shoulders straightened, and happiness sparked in his eyes. Cayden gave his brother a one-armed hug since he still held a plate of food. "You made it."

"Of course I did. I'm so proud of you." He sounded slightly out of breath when he reached them, like he'd run into the building.

"Thought you were going to be a no-show."

"Sorry I'm late. Work ran over." Dane had swooped his black hair off his forehead, highlighting his gorgeous eyes and chiseled bone structure. He was dressed in business-casual attire, a polo shirt, and fitted dress pants that many would find distracting in an office setting. He was only a few inches taller than Cayden and wore more muscle on his frame. Sawyer got a whiff of a spicy cologne that smelled expensive when Dane stepped back from hugging his brother. He held Cayden at arm's length, scrutinizing him up and down. "You good? Everything okay?"

"Yeah, I'm good."

"Who's this, Cay?" Royce asked.

"This is my big brother, Dane," the cadet replied proudly, looping his free arm around his brother's shoulders.

"Dane," Royce said, extending his hand. "It's good to meet you. I'm so glad you could make it."

The kid plastered a smile on his face when they shook hands, but it seemed forced since Sawyer had seen the real thing when he hugged his brother. "Cay was so excited when he got accepted into the Explorer program. I know he's going to do great things. I'm really proud of him."

Royce smiled and said, "He's already shown early signs of leadership and excellent character assessment."

Dane looked at his brother, and the genuine smile returned. "That's great to hear."

Royce introduced Dane to Sawyer, then offered the guy something to eat. "We ordered so much food, and I don't want to take home the leftovers."

"Thank you, but I already have plans." Dane turned to his brother and said, "Can we talk for a few minutes?"

Tension rose between them, but Cayden shrugged. "Yeah, sure."

The brothers moved to the far side of the room, and it was impossible not to glance in their direction every few seconds. "What's their story?" Sawyer asked.

"Their mother is battling late-stage cancer," Royce said. "Her prognosis isn't good, and I get the impression that the boys only have each other to get through it."

"Damn, that's awful." Sawyer knew all too well what kind of havoc cancer could wreak on a family. He looked at the brothers in time to see Dane hand his younger brother an envelope. Cayden shook his head, not wanting to take it, but Dane shoved it in his hand and closed his fingers around it. The cadet tucked the envelope inside his uniform jacket. "Did Cayden tell you this?"

"No, but Jason did." Royce's oldest nephew had just graduated from high school. He'd talked about becoming an Explorer cadet at one point but had changed his mind when he got serious about his art. Jason's hard work had earned him a coveted spot at Savannah College of Art and Design. "Jason is best friends with Dane, even though he's a little closer to Cayden's age," Royce explained.

"Is there anything we can do to help them?"

"I don't know yet. Jason said the brothers are a little prickly about accepting anything they perceive as handouts, so I will have to tread carefully."

"Male pride will be the ruin of us all," Sawyer teased.

Royce looked over Sawyer's left shoulder and narrowed his eyes. "I think we have bigger concerns to contend with right now."

Sawyer angled his body and noticed the gathering around Alec had grown to include the groupies he'd seen lingering in the hallway. *Just freaking great.* Alec's gaze strayed from his flock and landed on the Sutton brothers. Someone asked a question that yanked his attention back to the group, but Sawyer noted his gaze kept straying back to Cayden and Dane. But why? Was it because they weren't enamored with him? The brothers hugged quickly before Dane left, and Sawyer observed Alec tracking his movement until someone thrust a book at him to sign.

"Last one," Alec said. "I didn't mean to hijack the night." He smiled apologetically in Royce's direction, but then his eyes widened when he spotted Sawyer. "Excuse me, everyone. I need to speak to my new crime-solving partner."

Royce growled when Alec started toward them. The sound made Sawyer's heart flutter, but he desperately wanted to avoid a confrontation.

Leaning into his husband, Sawyer whispered, "Save that for when we get home, hot stuff."

Royce's gaze glittered with dark promise when it shifted back to him, and Sawyer hoped he'd headed trouble off at the pass.

Alec reached them, a friendly smile on his face and a hand out-stretched to Royce. "You must be the husband Sawyer can't stop talking about."

Royce gripped the hand hard enough to make Alec wince. "And you must be the one who can't take no for an answer."

Sawyer chuckled uneasily. So much for his efforts to prevent a confrontation.

Alec pulled his hand back and tried to look sheepish, but he just looked like a pompous asshole. He sucked air through his teeth, then said, "Yeah, guilty. I was just so excited to be here, and then Sawyer mentioned the Explorer's open house. I just thought it would make perfect material for the podcast. SPD will play a major role in our investigation, so why not tell the world about the amazing opportunities here for future LEOs?"

"That's not a decision for you to make," Sawyer said before Royce could respond. Alec was his problem, and he needed to take firm control of the situation before he caused actual damage. "Our contract outlined what access you would have at the precinct, and that didn't include the Explorer Academy."

Alec threw up both hands in surrender. "You're right. I apologize for intruding, even though open houses are public events."

Did this guy want to challenge Sawyer to a duel on semantics? Fine. He opened his mouth to refute Alec's arrogance, but he got a better idea when his gaze snagged on Cory the Super Fan lingering nearby. "Hey, Cory," Sawyer said, waving him over to join the conversation. The guy practically bounded over like a puppy. "Have you met your hero yet?" Okay, Sawyer worried he'd laid it on too thick until Alec straightened his posture and beamed a smile so bright that Cory tripped over his own two feet. He stumbled into Alec, who caught him by the shoulders and held him upright.

"I haven't had the pleasure yet," Alec said. "I'm always happy to meet a fan."

A hot blush crept up Cory's neck. "So sorry about that. I'm not usually this clumsy."

"We all trip up sometimes," Alec said.

"This is Cory Sands, and he's one of our finest forensic science technicians," Sawyer said before turning to Royce. "Cory has given presentations to your students before, right?"

"Every year," Royce replied. "Cory is engaging with the kids, and he makes forensic science look exciting."

"Because it is," Cory said. "And I have amazing material for the students this year."

"I'd like to hear all about it." Alec's gaze traveled the length of Cory's body, appreciation darkening his gaze.

Cory's eyes widened. "You would?"

"Absolutely. Maybe you could give me a tour of the academy's facilities too?" Alec looked at Royce for approval.

"Go right ahead," Royce replied, gesturing with his hand for them to proceed. "The event is open to the public, after all."

Alec and Royce locked gazes, but luckily, Cory's enthusiasm drew Alec's attention away before he could clap back and make things worse. "I'll catch you later."

"You'll catch me Monday morning at eight thirty and not a minute before," Sawyer told him firmly. "Have I made myself clear?"

Full lips formed a smirk. "Crystal."

Cory led Alec out of the community room, passing by the little fan club without so much as a wave or an introduction.

"Looks like Cory forgot all about his groupie friends now that he's rubbing elbows with the celebrity," Sawyer said.

"We have bigger fish to fry," Royce replied. "Or steam for those more health-conscious."

"I know."

"That guy is trouble," Royce stated.

"I know."

"This won't end well."

Sawyer wanted to deny it. He truly did, but only a heavy sigh escaped his lips. He met Royce's loving gaze and said, "I know."

CHAPTER THREE

MEOW.

Royce kept his gaze forward and told himself not to make eye contact as he shoved a piece of prosciutto into his mouth and chewed.

Meow.

"No. There's nothing for you to eat inside the refrigerator. It's gross human food." Sharp teeth grazed the back of his calf in warning. Royce could give Bones a tiny sliver of meat or end up with a bloody stump. "Fine. But don't tell on me."

Yip. Yip. Yip.

"That goes for you too," Royce told Dolly. He tore off the tiniest pieces he could get away with and fed them to his demanding animals, who immediately ran into the living room with their treasures. "And you better disguise the smell of pricey deli meats on your breath with kibble," he called after them before eating another piece of prosciutto. "Damn, that's good."

Royce tucked the bottles of beer and sparkling water in the crook of his elbow before grabbing the mini charcuterie board from the refrigerator. He closed the door and smiled at the grainy black-and-white image held in place with a pink magnetic picture frame. They said they wouldn't put Lil Plum's portrait on the refrigerator until after they made their big announcement, but they'd changed their minds after they returned home from the open house. Alec Bishop hadn't just crashed the event; the smarmy bastard had left an oil slick of dread in his wake that no amount of Dawn dish soap could clean. Sawyer had looked like a whipped dog after a private conversation with Mendoza, and Royce had wanted to put a smile on his face. They'd had to settle for a magnetic chip clip as Lil Plum's first accessory on Wednesday evening, but Royce had found a prettier frame at a baby boutique store the next day at lunch.

And the trick had seemed to work. He and Sawyer had kept to their routine of working hard and loving harder for the rest of the week, avoiding any conversation that could've led to Alec Fuckface Bishop. They'd spent most of their free time talking about their dreams and what their lives would look like in a year. Though Sawyer had tried to hide it, Royce noted a subtle shift in his husband's demeanor as the weekend progressed.

He'd woken to an empty bed on Sunday morning, something that only happened if one of them was out of town. Instead of sleeping in and making lazy love with Royce, Sawyer had gotten up early to take care of their pets and work out. Royce had found him covered in sweat and trembling from head to toe from his effort in their home gym. And yeah, he'd led Sawyer back to their bathroom and lathered him with soap and adoration, but he still hadn't relaxed.

By Sunday evening, Sawyer's handsome face was tight with tension, and Royce felt powerless to help. The solution was obvious to him, but he didn't want to argue with Sawyer about backing out of the arrangement with Alec. Royce was certain their legal team could point to multiple instances where Alec had already violated their contract, but Sawyer wouldn't want to hear it. His sexy, stubborn man was determined to fix the problems and honor his obligations.

Royce slid the patio door shut and made his way to the massive outdoor canopy bed he'd purchased for Sawyer's birthday. The head of the frame tilted up at a few different angles or lay flat, and they'd taken full advantage of every option, as well as the easy-clean mattress fabric. The bed came with sheer, white curtains that billowed beautifully in the breeze, but Royce had secured them to the bedposts after they'd gotten tangled up in them more than once. He'd placed several battery-powered lanterns on the patio around the bed and strung fairy lights along the top rail to ramp up the romance. The effort had been worth it, especially since Sawyer seemed relaxed for the first time all day. Halfway to his destination, Royce stopped dead in his tracks to admire the most stunning vista he'd ever seen.

The sky was an ombré wash of blues as dusky twilight surrendered to nightfall, making the perfect backdrop for the warm glow emanating from the bed and the gloriously naked man stretched on top of it. Damn, Karma must really love him. Sawyer reclined there like a god, one arm tucked under his head, waiting to be fanned and fed grapes. Every inch of his golden skin was perfect, even the burn scars on his chest he hated. Sawyer's free hand lazily trailed over his lower abdomen, drawing attention to his semi-erection. It took all the effort Royce possessed to keep from dropping the snacks and drinks or falling into the pool as he navigated a path back to Sawyer.

"Weren't you wearing swim shorts when I left?" They were the tiniest and tightest piece of fabric Royce had ever seen, so "shorts" was a stretch in the same way the material strained to contain his husband's cock and balls.

Sawyer's mouth curved into a smirk, and he opened one eye. "Do you want me to put them back on? I tossed them over there some-where." He pointed to a shadowy corner of the patio.

"Get serious." Royce set the drinks and snacks on the mattress next to Sawyer. He shoved his swim trunks down his legs and tossed them into the castoff corner. "I much prefer to feed you naked."

Sawyer opened both eyes and smiled. "You prefer to do every-thing naked."

"Only with you."

"You didn't have to go to so much trouble to cheer me up," Sawyer said. But the gesture had already smoothed some of his rougher edges. "A fancy salmon dinner followed by a relaxing swim, and now this." Sawyer plucked a Kalamata olive off the plate. He brought it to his mouth and turned eating the fruit into an art of seduction by sucking the juice from the pit opening before pushing it between his puckered lips. "Mmmm. So good. Perfect amount of salty."

Royce plucked a red grape from the pile and held it to Sawyer's lips. "This should be the right amount of sweet."

Sawyer smirked and said, "Just like you." He bit into the fruit, and juice dribbled onto his lip, inviting Royce to lean forward and lick it off. Passion flared in Sawyer's dark gaze as he fed the other half of the grape to Royce. "Come down here."

Royce shook his head and moved to the foot of the bed. "Not yet. Eat your snack and let me take care of you."

"You've been doing that all day. Let me pamper you."

Sitting on the edge of the mattress, Royce reached for the foot nearest to him. He dug two thumbs into the arch and smiled when Sawyer's eyes rolled back into his head, and he dropped the chunk of sharp cheddar cheese back onto the tray. Royce increased the pressure and circled his thumbs. "I'm taking care of you first."

Sawyer closed his eyes and practically melted into the mattress. "I want to object, but…"

"You won't." Royce lifted the leg and pressed a kiss to his ankle. "You'll let me do whatever I want because I always know what you need."

"Mmmm."

"Let me hear you say it."

Sawyer's lashes fluttered with the effort it took to open his heavy eyelids even halfway. "You always know what I need, because the only thing I need is you." His eyes drifted shut once more when Royce worked his thumbs toward the ball of his foot.

"You better eat your snack," Royce said. "It's going to take me a long time to work my way up to your cock. You'll need the sustenance for the blow job I'm about to give you."

Sawyer forced his eyes open and reached for a handful of dates and nuts. "In that—*oh, my god*—case." He trembled and watched Royce with wide-eyed wonder. "Wow. That felt like a mini orgasm. What did you push?"

Royce shrugged. "Don't know, but I feel like I need to tattoo an *X* on here to mark the spot." He shifted his left thumb over to join the right and pressed deeper. "Is this good?" Sawyer sucked in a sharp breath, and his dick jerked. "Wonder if I could make you come just from this?"

"Yes." The word came out as a needy whimper that went straight to Royce's groin. "It certainly feels like you could," Sawyer said. "And I just might let you."

"Let me?" Royce cocked his head to the side and studied the smug expression on his husband's face. "Baby, where's the fun in that?" He shifted his massaging thumbs lower and earned a delicious pout.

"Please."

Royce shook his head. "Eat your snack."

"Alone? Where's the fun in that?" Sawyer plucked a piece of dried fruit from the board and extended it to him.

Royce wasn't sure what it was, and he didn't really care as long as it wasn't prunes. He had big plans, and he didn't want those little fuckers to get in the way. Lowering Sawyer's foot onto the mattress, Royce leaned forward enough to accept the offering. He chewed the apricot slowly, savoring the balance of sweet and tart. Sawyer sat up and captured Royce's face in both hands before he could pull away.

"Come down here with me."

Royce kissed Sawyer, teasing his lips open with his tongue and sweeping inside his mouth, experiencing the salty and sweet notes from his snack. He'd only meant to kiss Sawyer and lay him back down, but he could never resist the rich taste of his husband and followed Sawyer to the mattress. Hip to hip and heart to heart, Royce's hands roamed over the body he knew better than his own, retracing the map of pleasure he'd previously marked. Each shiver, groan, or hitch of breath felt as familiar to Royce as his own heartbeat, and yet he felt like each journey led to a fresh discovery. A new freckle to kiss, an erogenous zone to explore, and sometimes even muscle aches to ease. Royce wasn't just along for the adventure; he was the freaking captain.

Tearing his mouth free, Royce stared into the eyes of the only person who'd seen his truth and taught him how to revel in it. Sawyer had lovingly glued each fragment of Royce's broken heart together and declared it a work of art, even though the fissures still showed and the glue had dripped over the edges in places. And Royce would battle to the end of the world for this man. "We've spent so much time thinking about what our lives will look like next year that we risk missing out on all the little miracles along the way."

Sawyer shifted a hand into Royce's hair and massaged his scalp.

The urge to close his eyes and purr like Bones was strong, but he didn't want to lose the connection with the chocolate-brown gaze he adored so much. "There's nothing small about the miracle pressing against my pelvis."

Royce snorted and nipped his bottom lip. "Don't distract me because you know I'm right. I never want to lose sight of this—of us." He pressed his finger to Sawyer's lips when they parted on a denial. "And we will. It's only human nature. With demanding careers and a kid, one of us is always going to draw the short straw." And Royce would be a complete liar if he didn't admit that the idea terrified him more than a little. "Just promise me we'll always find our way back to one another."

Sawyer tugged his head down until their mouths were a hairbreadth away. "Easiest promise I can make." Their lips met to seal their vow, soft and tentative at first. The slick glide of their tongues ramped up the intensity and drove away any thoughts except how they'd satisfy one another.

"Uncle Royce!" The urgent voice belonged to his oldest nephew, Jason. "You back there?" And it drew closer.

Royce scrambled off the canopy bed and frantically scanned the patio for their shorts. A tall privacy fence surrounded their pool, so Jason would have to climb onto something to peer into the backyard. Or open the gate. Damn, had he closed it after mowing the lawn? "Yeah, Jay," Royce called out. "I'm here. Hang on a minute."

Sawyer hunkered down and duckwalked over to the castoff corner. He looked like he was dodging a hail of bullets, which Royce might've found funny if they weren't minutes away from potentially exposing themselves.

"I've been calling and texting for an hour." The gate rattled as Jason tugged on it. Luckily, Royce had remembered to lock it after working in the yard. "I need to talk to you right now. It's an emergency."

Royce's heart skipped a beat as the many possibilities crossed his mind, each one more frightening than the one before it. A pair of swim shorts hit him in the face, interrupting his mini meltdown. He didn't even look to see if they were right side out as he tugged them on. Jason's abrupt appearance had dumped ice water on his arousal, so at least that was one less thing to worry about. "You good?" Royce asked over his shoulder as he crossed the patio to the gate.

"Uh, yeah. I think so." Sawyer's voice sounded strained, but he didn't stop to investigate the reason.

Royce shoved the bolt to the left and swung the gate open.

"Finally!" Jason said. He took two steps forward and then lurched to an abrupt stop. "What the hell are you wearing? And gross, dude. Beastie and the Boys are trying to escape." Jason looked beyond him to the romantic scene on the patio. His face turned bright red. "Um, oops."

Royce looked down and realized he'd put on Sawyer's micro swim shorts instead of his own. They were inside out and hiked up on one side, where a testicle was hanging halfway to freedom. The waistband hung so low on Royce's hips that his dick was seconds away from bursting out over the top. Turning his back to Jace, he readjusted the ridiculous shorts as best he could before meeting his nephew's embarrassed gaze. "What's up? You said it was an emergency."

Jason averted his eyes and scuffed his shoe back and forth over the concrete. "I'm sorry I interrupted."

"Don't worry about it." Sawyer's kind voice pulled Royce's attention to him again. Damn, he loved that man. "Let's go inside. You can hang with Dolly and Bones while we get dressed."

Jason nodded without making eye contact, then followed them into the house. They left him in the living room with the pets and hurried down the hallway. Sawyer collapsed against their closed bedroom door and doubled over with laughter, pointing in his direction.

Royce placed both hands on his hips and glared at Sawyer, but that only made him laugh harder. He looked down at his crotch and noticed that the brief walk to their bedroom had completely dislodged a testicle, and the head of his dick had escaped the low-riding waistband. Royce shoved the offending garment to the ground and stomped on it. The fit only made Sawyer howl harder at the situation. He slid to the floor as if his legs couldn't hold him any longer. "How the hell do you get your cock and balls into that stupid thing?"

Sawyer panted for breath. "Beastie and the Boys. God, I love that kid."

Royce didn't want to laugh at the situation, but Sawyer's unabashed delight was contagious. "You did that on purpose, didn't you?"

Sawyer laughed even harder and could only shake his head.

Royce moved to the dresser and removed underwear, shorts, and a T-shirt. "The kid didn't run screaming into the night, so he must have serious reasons for being here." He'd said it was an emergency, but teenagers often exaggerated the urgency of situations. Running out of chips and pizza constituted a disaster for some of them. But not Jason. "We might have to pay for his therapy," Royce said as he pulled on his underwear and shorts.

Sawyer pushed up from the floor and made his way over. "The kid is too levelheaded for that." More reason for them to get back to the living room. Sawyer pressed a firm kiss to his lips. "Go. I'm right behind you."

Royce hurried back to Jason, who waited for him with a lapful of dog and cat. "Can I get you anything?"

"No, I'm good." He kept his gaze on the animals as he petted them. "I feel kind of stupid now that I've taken a few minutes to calm down. I'm probably overreacting." He looked up then. "Sorry I ruined your night."

Royce dropped into the chair across from Jason. "You haven't ruined anything, and I'd rather you tell me what brought you here so we can work through it together."

"You're going to think I'm stupid."

Royce shook his head. "I can guarantee I won't."

"I might get someone I care about in trouble." Jason's shoulders slumped under the weight of his worry. "They're a good person doing something they shouldn't, but only to help the people they love."

"You can trust me. What's wrong, Jaybird?"

The nickname made Jason smile, but it didn't linger. "I think something bad happened to Dane."

Royce thought back to the handsome young man who'd shown up to support Cayden at the open house. Something poked at his brain until he remembered the awkward exchange between the brothers when Dane had tried to hand Cayden an envelope. They'd had words, not heated but still intense, and Cayden had eventually capitulated. What was in the envelope? Money? What illegal acts had Dane committed to give his brother the money? Drugs? Burglaries? Sex work? Hot cars?

Sawyer entered the room before Royce could press him further. "Jason, do you want anything to eat or drink?"

"No, thanks."

Sawyer sat in the empty chair beside Royce. "What did I miss?"

"Remember the guy named Dane from the open house?" Royce asked.

Sawyer nodded. "Cayden's older brother."

"Did Royce tell you about their mom?" Jason asked.

"Yes," Sawyer replied. "I'm sorry they're going through such a tough time."

"Their mom, Nina, is hanging on by the thinnest thread. She's doing it for them. Their only income is the monthly pittance she's getting from the state. Her employer fired her as soon as her illness made it impossible for her to work consistently. If she dies, there's no one to take care of Cayden. Their dad split fifteen years ago and hasn't paid a lick of child support since. Hell, they don't even know if he's alive. Dane and Cay don't have any relatives to help them, and Nina's afraid the state won't allow Dane to be Cay's guardian." Jason buried his head in Bones' neck for a few minutes before meeting their gaze again. "Especially if they know what he's doing to keep food on the table. All Cay and Dane have is each other."

"How can we help?" Sawyer asked.

"Jason had just told me he thinks something bad has happened to Dane. It sounds like he's been doing something illegal to help make ends meet." Royce turned back to Jason. "I need you to tell me everything if I'm going to help you out, okay?"

Jason held his gaze for several seconds before nodding. "Dane's an escort. He hooks up with men for money."

Royce felt like someone had punched him in the stomach. Sex work was extremely dangerous. "And you think Dane has run into trouble?"

"Yes," Jason whispered.

"Why?" Sawyer asked.

"No one has heard from him since Wednesday night. I know that doesn't seem like a long time, and he's an adult who can do what he wants, but Dane doesn't go dark for more than a few days at a time. Not with his mom so sick."

"He handed an envelope to Cayden on Wednesday night at the open house," Royce said. "I assume it had money in it."

"Two thousand dollars," Jason said.

Royce whistled in surprise. "That's a lot of money."

"Dane works with high-end clients. He said they paid better and were less risky."

A mistake many people had learned the hard way. Privileged people wanted to keep their status, and getting caught with an escort could cost them penalties they weren't willing to pay. Had someone viewed Dane as an expendable risk? The chilling thought sent a shiver down his spine.

"Could he have gone out of town with a client?" Royce asked.

Jason shook his head vigorously. "You don't understand. Nina had a meeting to discuss her hospice options on Friday morning. Dane was supposed to be there, but he didn't show. He didn't text or call to explain why. His phone had gone straight to voicemail like it's dead or turned off." Jason swallowed hard and silently implored Royce with moody gray eyes so much like his own. "Nina tried to file a police report, but they're not taking her seriously. They gave her some song and dance about adults being allowed to walk away from their lives if they want to. The guy told her that Dane might've run off because he can't accept that she was dying."

"Fuck, that was harsh," Sawyer said. "I hope she got his name or badge number so we can report his shitty behavior to his superior officer."

"Maybe," Jason said.

"Is there any chance Dane could have walked away from everything?" Royce asked.

"Hell no." Jason's resolute expression never wavered. "Dane has attended every medical appointment and treatment with Nina. Does that sound like someone who would peace out when she needed him most?"

"No," Royce admitted.

"I've been in Dane's shoes," Sawyer said. "And you don't always think or behave rationally when someone you love is dying." He held up his hands when it looked like Jason was going to protest. "I'm not saying he ran off or that you shouldn't be worried. I'm just explaining that grief brings out unpredictable reactions from people."

Jason pursed his lips and nodded. "I'll give you that. I can't imagine what's going through his mind right now, and he's sure as hell not talking about it." Jason tapped his chest. "But I feel it here." He raised his hand and tapped his temple. "And here. Something is really wrong. My friend is in danger or…" His voice trailed off when he couldn't finish the thought.

The more Jason talked about Dane, the more Royce believed his nephew was right. Sex work was dangerous on a good day, but high levels of stress had likely impaired Dane's judgment and put him at a higher risk for harm. "This is what we're going to do," Royce said. "You're going to call Cayden and tell him that you and I are coming over."

Jason shook his head. "He won't like that. Their house is a mess right now. Nina won't want you to see it."

"You came here for my help, and we're going to do things my way," Royce said. "Tell them I don't care how clean their house is. I just want to help them find Dane. We can talk on the front porch if they'd feel more comfortable."

Jason took a deep breath and nodded. "Okay. I'll call."

It was fully dark by the time Royce and Jason parked at the curb in front of the Suttons' home. A single bare bulb next to the front door cast a small circle of dim light onto the covered porch, its wattage no match for the inky night pressing in. The bulb flickered a few times as if surrender was imminent, but the light steadied and seemed to glow a little brighter when Royce turned off his SUV. He wasn't one to look for signs from the universe, but he wondered if that resilient light mirrored the will of the people living inside the home. Cancer was the formidable, heartless foe that just kept coming, and Nina's spirit refused to give up until she found out what happened to her son. There was no amount of bracing that would prepare Royce for the heartache he was about to witness. The best he could do was open himself to it and help them any way he could.

Jason reached for the door handle but stopped. "Watch your step on the front walk. There are a lot of cracks, and the concrete is uneven."

Royce reached over and placed a hand on his nephew's shoulder. "Have I ever told you how proud I am of the young man you've turned out to be?"

Jay shrugged like it was no big deal, but Royce saw a hint of a smile tug at his lips. "You're so sappy, Uncle Ro." He reached for the door handle again. "But thanks. I think you're pretty badass too."

Royce unbuckled his seat belt and stepped out of the vehicle. "Well, that was never in doubt."

Jason waited for him, and they navigated the uneven pavement together. "Told you," he said once they reached the circle of light.

"I can easily fix that for them," Royce said as he knocked on the front door. While they waited for someone to answer, Royce assessed the porch's condition and noted several rotten or warped boards. "And the porch."

Jason chuckled softly. "Please don't say anything. It will only make them feel bad."

"I won't." He'd just show up on Saturday morning and take care of it.

Footsteps quickly approached on the other side of the door. The knob turned, but the door didn't budge. The wood had probably swollen from the humidity.

"Going to fix that too?" Jason whispered.

Royce tapped two fingers against his temple. "It's going on the list."

Jason shook his head. "Don't make me regret this."

With a grunt, the door swung open so hard that Cayden stumbled back a few steps. Embarrassment crept up his neck and settled into his cheeks. "Hey, Jay. Um, hello, sir."

"I'm sorry to show up so late, but Jason told me you've had trouble filing a missing person report at the precinct."

"They wouldn't even take a report," Cayden said. "The first cop told us to wait forty-eight hours, so we did. We tried to file a second time, and that cop wouldn't take the report either. Gave us the same song and dance about Dane running off. It's making me rethink a career in law enforcement. I don't want to be that asshole someday."

"Then don't," Royce said. "There are going to be times where your hands are tied as a cop and you have limited options, but it's never okay to be an asshole to people. How about you invite me in so I can help, and you give my program a fair shake?"

Cayden's eyes looked suspiciously moist when he cleared his throat. "Yes, sir. Come in. Please excuse the mess." He stepped aside for them to enter, and Royce gestured for Jason to go first.

"Don't worry about that," he told his cadet. "I'm here to help however I can. You name it."

"Do you know how to fix a dishwasher?" Cayden asked. "Ours died, and now, everything we own is dirty. I'm trying to keep up with stuff, but…"

"I'll look at it," Royce said. "I might not be able to fix it tonight if I need a part from the hardware store, but Jason and I can help you clean the kitchen. Right, kid?"

"Sure." Jason had done more than his fair share of dishes over the years, with Dru working long hours to make ends meet.

Cayden turned redder. "I can't ask you to do dishes."

"You didn't," Jason said. "We volunteered."

"Cay," a frail voice called from somewhere in the house. "Is Dane back home?"

"No, Mama." Cayden hung his head. "It's Jason and his uncle, Sergeant Locke." He stepped closer to Royce and lowered his voice. "I told her you were coming, but she's forgotten already. They've put her on pretty strong meds to keep her comfortable."

Royce settled his hand on Cayden's shoulder. "I'm truly sorry for everything you're going through."

The young man's head slumped forward, and his thin body trembled. "I just don't know what to do. It's so hard to see my mom like this. Dane has carried the burden for the past year and a half. Maybe he's really had enough."

"No way," Jason hissed. "You know better, Cay. He'd never leave you to deal with this alone. He'd never abandon Nina." Jason shifted his weight and rubbed the back of his neck. "Look, it's probably easier to think Dane hit the road than accept the alternative, but he's out there somewhere, and I won't leave him. We have to bring him home… no matter what."

Royce wanted to caution Jason not to leap to conclusions, but statistics didn't favor a good outcome. There were a few scenarios that could explain Dane's absence, and most of them weren't good. "Let's get started."

Cayden really didn't want to show them deeper into the house, but he finally gave in and led them down the hallway. Most of the rooms they passed were pitch-dark, but the musty odor of dust and neglect was ripe in the air. Cayden flipped on the kitchen light, and Royce's heart lurched. Piles of dirty dishes covered every surface, and trash overflowed onto the floor. Empty pizza boxes and carryout boxes

formed columns around the room. The problems had started long before the dishwasher broke. Christ, what the hell had these boys and
their mother lived through, and for how long? The gravity of the situation settled on Royce's shoulders like a leaden blanket. He wouldn't
allow Cayden to live in these conditions, and he didn't care what ob-
stacles stood in his way.

A broken sob penetrated his thoughts, and Royce hooked an arm
around Cayden's neck to pull him into a tight hug. Great big, hiccup-
ping breaths racked the boy's thin body. "Don't know what to do. I've
tried so hard. I need Dane."

Royce held him harder as tears leaked through his shirt. "I've got
you now, Cay. You hear me?" The devastated kid nodded against his
shoulder. "We're going to get through this. One step at a time."

Jason turned toward the sink, but not before Royce saw the tears
streaming down his face. He opened a few cabinets until he found a
box of trash bags. He pulled one free, snapped it in the air a few times
to open it, and began tossing the obvious trash away.

Cayden pulled in a deep breath and stepped out of Royce's embrace. He wiped away his tears with the back of his hand and assessed
the room. "Okay. One step."

Royce nodded. "What have you done to find Dane so far?"

"I called every hospital in a seventy-mile radius and talked to
Dane's friends," Cayden said. "Struck out every time."

"Friends other than Jason?" Royce asked.

"Jason and two others," Cayden replied. "Dane didn't have time
to maintain friendships, so the other guys hadn't talked to him in several months."

"He tried to blow me off too, but I wouldn't let him," Jason said.

"Do either of you know if Dane worked independently or for
someone else?" The guys exchanged a glance and shrugged. "Do you

know if he developed friendships with other escorts?" Royce asked. "They often form buddy circles and develop safety protocols to look out for one another."

"He's mentioned someone a few times," Jason said, not looking up from his task. "Only by a nickname, but I think I know a place to start."

"See if you can get them to talk to me," Royce said. "Be clear that I'm not looking to make any trouble for anyone. I just want to find Dane."

"Okay."

"What about Dane's electronics?" Royce asked. "Phone, tablets, or a computer? Would you know any of his passwords? We might be able to trace his steps. We won't be able to get a warrant just based on the little information we have right now, but if we could get into his accounts, we could track his movements."

"Dane doesn't sleep here every night," Cayden said. "I think he feels weird being around mom after he spends time with clients."

"Any idea where he's crashing?"

"Probably with the same guy I'm going to talk to," Jason said. "If Dane left stuff behind, it would be at his place."

"Can you try to get in touch with him now?" Royce asked.

Jason put the trash bag down and retrieved his phone. He nodded toward the hallway. "I'll step outside and call him."

Once they were alone, Royce switched the conversation to the dishwasher. He'd already taken the bottom rack and the rotating sprayer out and identified the problem by the time Jason returned. A metal rivet from a steak knife had come loose and jammed up the circulation pump housing, causing the mechanism to burn up. "Easy fix. I just need to grab some replacement parts from the hardware store tomorrow." He looked at Jason. "Any news?"

His nephew shook his head. "I left a voicemail on his phone and tried to reach him on the socials. He'll get back to me as soon as he gets my messages."

"There's got to be more we can do," Cayden said.

"Have you put the information out on social media?" Royce asked.

Cayden shook his head. "Dane would be so pissed."

"Cay," Jason softly chided. "We can't afford to worry about that right now. Not if we hope to find him alive." Jason shot Royce a pleading look that begged him to promise it wasn't too late. While it was possible Dane was still alive, the odds weren't in his favor, and Royce wouldn't give his nephew or Cayden false hope.

"You start on the social media posts while Jason and I clean the kitchen," Royce instructed.

"Yes, sir."

It took almost two hours to wash and dry the dishes, empty the refrigerator of expired leftovers, and take out the trash. It was after eleven by the time Royce and Jason climbed back into the SUV.

"I wish we could've done more," Jason said. "This is so frustrating."

"Missing person cases are tough, especially when we don't even know where to start."

"What's next?" Jason asked.

"I'm going to make sure someone at the precinct starts an official missing person investigation for Dane." But Royce knew that wouldn't be nearly enough to help the family in crisis. "My classes don't start until Tuesday afternoon, so I'm going to take tomorrow off to handle Cayden and Nina's most pressing needs. Then we take things day by day." But how much time did Nina have left? And what would happen to Cayden?

"Dane's dead, isn't he?" Jason whispered.

The question hadn't caught Royce off guard because his nephew had always been mature for his age. Jason expected honesty from Royce, and he wouldn't let the kid down now. "I don't know."

"But you think so," Jason pushed.

Royce swallowed hard and met his nephew's wounded gaze. "It's the most common outcome in cases like these, but let's not lose hope."

Jason lowered his head and cried. Royce wished he could do or say something to make him feel better. When Jason was little, a trip to the ice cream parlor could fix most things. Two scoops of Cookie Monster ice cream on a sugar cone couldn't mend this kind of hurt. He blew out a shaky breath. "Thanks for being honest with me."

"Always." Royce glanced over at him before starting the vehicle. "I want you to feel safe to come to me with anything. I'm always going to be here for you."

"I know." Jason sniffled. "I love you, Uncle Ro."

Dru had done an amazing job of raising her sons, and Jason's willingness to express his emotions and show vulnerability was the greatest testament to that. She'd been the first to break the Locke mold and had done so at an early age because she had little people depending on her. It had taken Royce twice as long and required Sawyer's influence before he'd fully broken the chains holding him back.

"Love you too, kid."

Royce pulled away from the curb and headed home. The silence enveloping the vehicle was a palpable passenger with its own pulse. If what Jason said about Cayden's circumstances was correct, the kid was staring down a double barrel of heartbreak that Royce couldn't fathom. If someone didn't step up for Cay, he could end up in the foster system, and that didn't always work out so well for juveniles. Royce halted his catastrophizing before it turned into a downward spiral. There was no need to get ahead of himself. Get the facts first and then freak the fuck out.

"What's going to happen to Cay?" Jason asked when Royce pulled into his driveway. "You know, when this is all over."

"I don't have all the answers right now, Jaybird, but I promise he will not get lost in an overwhelmed system."

Jason's brows drew together. "How can you say that?"

"Because I will flex whatever clout I have to ensure it doesn't happen." Royce shut off the SUV and faced his nephew. "I've got Cayden from here on out."

"Thank you."

"Are you good?" Royce asked. "You're more than welcome to stay here tonight."

Jason's mouth quirked into a wry smile. "I think I've already crashed your plans enough for one night." He shook his head. "And I might be permanently scarred by what I saw." Jason's reference to Royce's Beastie and the Boys seemed like it happened a hundred years ago instead of a few hours. "But that is a sweet setup you have by the pool."

"Because I'm a smooth operator, kid."

"Gross," Jason grumbled as he removed his seat belt and reached for the door.

Royce chuckled as he exited the vehicle a moment later. He followed Jason to his car and pulled him into a hard hug. "Everyone should have a friend like you. The world would certainly be a better place."

"Thank you."

Royce stayed put in the driveway until Jason's taillights disappeared down the street. The house was dark and quiet when he went inside. Sawyer had likely gone to bed soon after he'd left with Jason. Flickering light spilled into the hallway from their bedroom, along with a familiar whirring sound. Royce shook his head and smiled when he walked into their room to find Sawyer, Bones, and Dolly sprawled across the bed while James and Dirt Reynolds worked their magic on a filthy rug on the television. Royce let the video play while he took a shower and repositioned his husband and fur children to reclaim a small strip of the bed. On the screen, James emptied the final bucket of water he'd vacuumed from the rug. It looked as clear as drinking water.

"Well, James, at least one of us had a happy ending tonight," Royce mumbled before turning the television off.

CHAPTER FOUR

N O MATTER HOW FAST SAWYER RAN ON THE TREADMILL, HE couldn't escape the tension pressing against his chest. The quicker his feet moved, the tighter his lungs felt. Instead of easing up, Sawyer doubled down. Exercise was his second-favorite stress reliever and usually very effective when his first choice, fucking his husband, wasn't an option. Since he'd left Royce sound asleep in their bed, Sawyer would have to rely on cardio to combat his growing anxiety over working with Alec. The dread had started on Sunday morning and would've ruined his favorite day of the week if not for Royce's over-the-top efforts to relax him. His husband's magic hands had nearly chased every bad thought from his head until Jason had interrupted them.

Once Sawyer was left to his own devices, his overactive brain had kicked into high gear, imagining every worst-case scenario involving Alec's time in Savannah. At one point, he'd envisioned losing his husband, his pets, and his career. It was the worst country song ever recorded, and the residual melancholy had forced Sawyer to take drastic measures to find relief. He hadn't fallen into the arms of another man, but another man's machine had charmed Sawyer into a state of calm.

Watching Dirt Reynolds tackle the world's filthiest rugs had relaxed him enough to fall asleep, but Sawyer's discontent invaded his dreams. He'd woken two hours before his alarm was due to go off and then glared at the clock and his slumbering husband as if they were the villains in his story. Bringing Alec on board was ultimately Sawyer's responsibility, and he'd suffer any and all consequences of an unhappy precinct and spouse. Mendoza had made the former crystal clear when he'd pulled Sawyer aside after the open house on Wednesday night. Royce had taken pity on him and hadn't mentioned Alec's name again, but Sawyer knew their truce wouldn't last…unless he took control of the situation as he'd promised to do. That thought had propelled him out of bed and into their home gym, but the peace he'd expected to find there still eluded him.

When black dots danced across his vision, Sawyer knew he needed to take a different approach. He slowed the treadmill to a brisk walk and went through his cooldown routine, raising his arms over his head to expand his rib cage for deeper breaths. He needed to get his head on right and stop giving Alec so much power. Sawyer held all the cards, and he got to play them as he saw fit. He slowed the treadmill again and adjusted his gait accordingly. Alec couldn't ruin his career and cause chaos in his personal life unless Sawyer let him. And so, he wouldn't.

That simple decision loosened the knot of tension gripping his chest. He cycled through some cleansing breaths and felt restored by the time he turned the treadmill off. A quick glance at the time revealed he had another hour before Royce would wake up, so Sawyer moved to the yoga mat to work the residual tension from his limbs.

He closed his eyes and went inward, connecting mind and body as he flowed through his morning salutations.

In this heightened state, Sawyer was attuned to the even cadence of his heart, the rhythmic rise and fall of his chest, and the stillness of his mind. So he was just as aware when those components of his well-being shifted, such as flared nostrils on his next inhalation, a quickening pulse, and the intense yearning that crashed his peace. The trifecta of sensations could only mean one thing.

"Your ass must be illegal in several states."

Sawyer transitioned from the downward dog into a table pose and met Royce's hungry gaze in the mirror. His husband stood in the doorway, wearing nothing but his underwear and a cocky grin. "No, but many states would like to ban what you do to it."

He added a little wiggle that drew Royce's immediate attention and a responding growl, yet he stayed put instead of pouncing on the invitation. Sawyer scanned the body he knew better than his own and noted the signs of stress he found in Royce's ramrod posture, the defensive way he crossed his arms over his chest, and his pinched-mouth expression. He recalled the reason Jason had come over the previous night and stood up.

"How'd it go with Cayden and his mom?"

Royce opened and shut his mouth a few times, but nothing came out. Mincing words wasn't his style, so things must've been as dire as Jason predicted.

Crossing the room, Sawyer cupped Royce's face and pressed a quick kiss against his tense lips. "We'll do whatever we can to help him."

Royce closed his eyes and swayed forward, crashing into Sawyer's embrace. "Cay is in such a bind," he said, then described the condition of the house and Nina's rapidly failing health. "And I have an awful feeling about Dane."

"Your opinion matters at the precinct, so use your influence for good," Sawyer said.

"Finding someone who will take Dane's disappearance seriously is my top priority," Royce replied. "Tara and I have everything ready for the first day of classes tomorrow, but I'll call her in a bit and let her know what's happening. I need to head back over to Cayden's house this morning. I promised to fix the dishwasher today, and I want to assess his overall living situation to see what else needs immediate attention." Royce rested his forehead against Sawyer's shoulder. "I'd hoped to be at the station today in case you needed a safe place to hide from Alec Bishop."

Sawyer groaned. "If you say his name two more times, he'll probably appear like Bloody Mary."

Royce lifted his head and nuzzled his nose against Sawyer's neck. "I really love it when you're sweaty."

"No, you enjoy making me sweaty."

Hot lips kissed a trail upward, not stopping until they reached Sawyer's mouth. Royce tasted like fresh mint and wicked fun. But all too soon, he pulled back and stared into Sawyer's eyes. "I caught you having another threesome with James and Dirt Vader last night."

Sawyer chuckled. "Guilty. It was the only way I could shut off my brain to sleep." He stroked a hand over Royce's bare chest. "Since you weren't home to tuck me in."

Tumultuous gray eyes softened in sympathy. "I hate how that Al—"

Sawyer silenced him with a hard kiss. "Please don't summon him and ruin the last two hours of peace I'll have for the duration of his stay in Savannah."

"I hate how *he* winds you up."

"Me too, but I'm in charge here." When Royce waggled his brows, Sawyer cocked his head to the side. "Well, not *here*. We're equal partners in our relationship. I meant at work and the case we'll be working on for the podcast. I won't dance around him and play nice to keep the peace. He'll do as I say, or the deal is off."

Royce snarled and growled playfully, but the air crackled with carnal energy. "Damn, my man is smoking hot when he's bossy." He gripped Sawyer's ass cheeks tightly. "Take me to bed, put me on my knees, and show me who's boss."

Sawyer cocked a brow. "Why wait?" He shoved Royce's underwear down and watched as the fabric landed on the floor. "Do you remember the first time I made you come?"

Royce's nostrils flared. "I only relive it every five seconds."

Sawyer slipped a hand between them and stroked Royce's hardening dick. "It was right in this room."

Royce nodded his head to the right. "Over on that leg curl bench. Want to relive the moment?"

"Huh-uh. I have other ideas for you this morning." Sawyer led Royce to the yoga mat and guided him to his knees. His husband leaned forward and buried his face in Sawyer's crotch, forgetting that he wasn't in charge. Sawyer cupped Royce's chin to hold him still. "I am going to shove your face somewhere else."

Royce dragged Sawyer's shorts and underwear off and tossed them out of the way. "Don't forget the lube before you pin my face to the mat and fuck the life out of me."

"I'd never forget that." Bending down to kiss his upturned mouth, Sawyer said, "And I'm going to fuck the life *into* you while you watch in the mirror." He stepped away to retrieve the lube and heard Royce shifting on the mat. When Sawyer turned back around, Royce was on his knees with his ass in the air. He'd pressed one side of his face against the mat and watched Sawyer's reaction in the mirror. "So eager." Royce had parted his legs just enough to expose his puckered entrance. "Perfection."

Meow.

Sawyer whipped around to find Bones watching them from the gym's threshold. "I didn't summon you, big guy." Sawyer retraced his steps and lovingly shooed the big feline into the hallway so he could shut the door.

"He's going to make you pay for that," Royce warned.

Sawyer dropped to his knees on the mat and dragged a finger along the crease between Royce's firm globes. "It will be so worth it." He tapped the crinkled rim but moved away when Royce pressed back against the caress to get penetration. "I'm in charge."

Royce moaned his frustration and wiggled his tight ass. "But you don't have time to draw this out since you need to leave for work soon."

"Not for another ninety minutes." He swirled his digit around and around Royce's puckered perfection. "I've got plenty of time."

"Not me," Royce said. "I might die if you don't—" His words snagged in his throat when Sawyer drizzled the lube over his rim. Royce's eyes closed, and a euphoric expression washed over his face. "Please, baby."

"Please what?"

"You know what I need."

"And I'll give it to you." Sawyer pressed the tip of his finger inside the tight ring and paused. "But I want to see your gorgeous eyes first." Royce's eyelids snapped open, and he locked his lusty gaze on Sawyer. "There's my man." He slid the slick digit all the way in, drawing a guttural groan from his man.

"Christ, that's good." Golden lashes fluttered, but Royce kept his eyes open and locked on Sawyer's face in the mirror.

"Watch the way I take you apart, first with my fingers and then with my dick."

Royce's lips quirked up. "I love it when you unleash this side of you."

Sawyer worked a second finger into him. Pleasure washed over Royce's face, and a blush bloomed across his bare skin. "That's right. Relax and open for me." Leaning over, he trailed kisses along Royce's spine, starting at his neck and working his way lower. "I want you to feel me for hours so you know who you belong to, but I don't want you to hurt."

Royce widened his legs and pushed his ass back. "You'll make it hurt so good."

Sawyer sank his teeth into Royce's left ass cheek. A surprised yelp melted into a needy moan. "Like that?"

"God, yes."

He stroked his hand over Royce's thigh, loving the quiver of muscle beneath his taut skin. Sawyer slipped his hand between Royce's legs to cup his balls and stroke his cock. "You want me so bad."

Royce snorted and rocked his hips to ride Sawyer's fingers. "Brilliant detective work."

Sawyer responded with a playful slap on Royce's ass. "Don't get cheeky, and do as I say."

"I'm yours to command."

Easing his fingers free of Royce's ass, Sawyer slicked his cock and leaned over Royce's back once more. Sawyer lowered his mouth to Royce's ear and whispered, "Watch me take you." Then he entered Royce with a powerful thrust that stole both their breath. When

Royce's eyelids drooped to half-mast, Sawyer fisted the back of his hair. Stormy gray eyes met his in the mirror. "Don't look away."

"Never."

Some worries he'd had the previous night bled into his lovemaking. The fear of losing Royce made him want to mark him that much harder. The force of his thrusts drove Royce up the mat, but he didn't have to wonder if he was going too hard. Royce challenged him to take more with a sexy smirk and rocked to meet Sawyer's thrusts. Curling over his back, Sawyer nuzzled against Royce's neck, wanting to sink his teeth into the corded muscle to mark him.

"Do it," Royce growled. Of course, he knew what Sawyer needed from him, but they still got razzed over a love bite he'd accidentally given Royce years ago. "But do it fast. Your perfect dick is pounding me just right."

Sawyer lowered his mouth below Royce's collar line and sucked his skin while plowing that ass like their lives depended on it.

"Sexy fucker," Royce groaned. "Hurts so good. Don't stop. Reach around and jerk me off."

"I'm in charge." Instead of ramping up the tempo, Sawyer straightened up and eased the pace. He withdrew his dick until only the head remained and then slid back in balls-deep.

Royce shivered hard when Sawyer's cock nudged his prostate once more. "Make me come."

"Or what?" Sawyer challenged. "Remember the heinous way you tormented me with that damn remote-controlled butt plug? I'm just giving you a tiny taste of that teasing."

Royce pushed up on his hands and rocked against Sawyer's next thrust. "Stop acting like you didn't love it. You came so hard you nearly blacked out." He reached for his dick with his right hand, but Sawyer blocked his attempt.

"I'm in charge of your pleasure." Sawyer used the momentum of his rocking hips to push Royce flat to the mat, driving his cock deeper inside the pert ass. "And I say not yet."

Royce writhed and moaned beneath him, using the friction of the yoga mat to his advantage. "Going to spunk all over your mat."

"And I'm going to flood your ass."

"Yes. Please." Royce stiffened beneath Sawyer, grunting as he found his release. His tight channel clamped around Sawyer's dick and triggered his climax.

Sawyer rutted against his man until he had nothing left to give and then collapsed on the mat beside Royce. "You just going to lie there in your jizz or what?"

Royce rolled onto his side, pressing his sticky pelvis against Sawyer's hip and resting his head on Sawyer's chest. "You light me up like a pinball machine every time. Bells ring, lights flash, and I always achieve the highest score."

Sawyer chuckled. "Sorry, I don't have a prize to hand out."

Royce lifted his head and rested his chin on Sawyer's chest. "You are my prize," he said. "Remember that when things go sideways with *that guy.*"

Sawyer's heart threatened to burst with love. "What kind of prize am I? Are we talking a Showcase Showdown from *The Price is Right* or a cheap metal ring from a gumball machine that turns your finger green in five minutes?"

"The Powerball and Mega Millions rolled into one." Royce pushed into a sitting position and looked at the mess they'd made. "Better get this cleaned up and get moving before we fall asleep in here. Christ, if you're late to work this morning…"

Sawyer sat up fast enough to make his head spin. "Mendoza will kill me."

Royce didn't deny it because he knew it was true. "You hit the shower. I'll take care of cleanup in aisle two, start the coffee, and make breakfast."

Sawyer didn't need Royce to tell him twice.

Sawyer whistled as he entered the precinct at a quarter to eight. Listening to an episode of *The Mel Robbins Podcast* during his drive to work had reminded him that he couldn't control other people. He was in charge of how he reacted to them and their bullshit. He hadn't miraculously cured his anxiety over the situation with a round of good sex, a tasty breakfast, and sage advice, but he would fake it until he made it. Holly and Topher were already in the CCU bullpen, loading their protective tactical gear from storage lockers into black bags. Sawyer's progress nearly flatlined on the spot because he couldn't assist them with their big takedown that morning.

Mendoza's mandate after the open house replayed in his mind. "I don't want Bishop roaming unsupervised in my precinct. Am I clear? Where he goes, you go too."

There was no way they'd make the four arrests and be back in time for him to intersect Alec. "Sorry, I won't be with you," Sawyer said.

"We've got this, Sarge," Toph replied.

Holly looked at him with a sympathetic smile. "We have a great team and a solid plan. Just be ready to look pretty in front of the media since they'll likely want a statement after the arrests."

Would Mendoza make Sawyer drag Alec to the podium with him, or would the chief give the statement to the reporters? A better idea landed. "This is your big bust, Holls, so it's only right that you talk to the press."

"By myself?"

Her surprise made Sawyer feel like a glory hound. Christ, maybe he had more in common with Alec than he realized. "I'm not taking credit for your work. Besides, I have babysitting duties, and I don't know where they'll lead me. Debrief Mendoza when you get back, and he will make the media arrangements."

Holly zipped up her bag and hoisted it over her shoulder. "But the camera loves you so much."

Sawyer waved her off. "Be safe. Stay alert."

Topher gave him a two-finger salute, and Holly tapped her heart before they left. And then it was just Sawyer in the silent bullpen. He unlocked the door to the conference room he set aside for the investigation. The case files, which they agreed to give Alec full access to, sat next to the whiteboards for Monica Horton and Jane Doe number one. Sawyer had locked the other three files away since the DNA results had ruled them out as Andrew Bishop's victims. The long table in the center of the room provided ample space for Alec and his two-person crew to work. He glanced at the clock and noted he had thirty minutes until his guests were due to arrive, so he reviewed everything he knew so far.

After Alec showed his ass last Wednesday evening, Sawyer focused his efforts on finding someone from Monica Horton's family who was willing to talk to him. He'd struck gold with Talia Atwood, Monica's first cousin, who now lived in Jacksonville. She'd been hesitant to talk about Monica at first. Her death had hit her family hard, but it also brought a lot of embarrassment when the media coverage mostly focused on her alleged sex work. Monica's family had also been unimpressed by the department's handling of her case, and they'd refused to engage with each new detective who took a swing at solving her murder.

Sawyer wished he could say that times had changed enough for the media and their police department to handle similar cases differently, but he only had to recall Jason's desperation the previous night to realize that the needle hadn't moved far enough. Cayden had Royce in his corner, and he wouldn't ease up until he got answers. And Sawyer must've said the right thing or struck the correct tone with Talia because she agreed to a Zoom call on her lunch break.

A shoe scuffed against the tile floor with a loud squeak, and Sawyer ducked his head outside the conference door. Footsteps grew louder in the corridor, and muffled voices turned into an audible conversation as Alec and company approached the bullpen. Sawyer forced a friendly smile on his face and stepped out of the conference room.

"I made a real ass of myself last week," Alec said, "and I'm nervous about our reception this morning."

"I'm sure those donuts will go a long way toward making amends," Marina Woods, Alec's producer, said. Sawyer recognized her no-nonsense tone from their meeting in Denver.

A masculine chuckle rumbled down the corridor and made Sawyer smile. "Playing into stereotypes by offering donuts to a cop could backfire and piss him off even more." Sawyer assumed the new voice belonged to Ricky Nunez, the videographer Alec told him about.

"Fuck," Alec hissed. "You might be right. We should probably turn around, pack up, and get out of town before they run us out."

"Oh, stop it," Marina said. "I was there when you met with Detective Key in Denver, and you guys got along very well. How badly could you have fucked things up already?"

"My behavior was a toss-up between petulant toddler and arrogant asshole. I can't decide." Alec sighed.

"So, a petulant asshole," Ricky said.

Alec snorted. "Pretty much."

"Well, we're here now," Marina said. "Just apologize for whatever you did or said and ask for a clean slate. Detective Key seems like a reasonable man."

Sawyer crossed the bullpen and poked his head out of the door. "Only after I've had my first cup of coffee, Marina."

The trio stopped suddenly and looked at him with a variety of expressions on their faces. Alec blushed with mortification and dropped his gaze to the three huge pastry boxes in his arms. Ricky grinned impishly and readjusted the equipment bags slung over his shoulder. Marina's arched brow begged the question: *And have you?*

"Luckily, I'm on my second cup this morning." Sawyer gestured for them to come inside before ducking back into the room. "And the stereotype that cops love donuts exists for a reason," he told Ricky. "Some in the precinct might have bitchy thoughts while they devour your gift, but most won't air their grievances for fear you might take the donuts back. And the ones who get snarly are hard to take seriously with powdered sugar on their shirts or jelly smears on their faces."

Ricky's dark eyes shimmered with glee as he rubbed his hands together. "I like you. This is going to be fun."

"I'm hoping our time here is going to be productive," Marina said. "And award winning." That latter part added a slight flush to her cheeks. Sawyer hated to break it to her, but accolades were the last thing on his mind.

"And I just want the truth," Alec said. "No matter the cost."

Something about Alec's tone implied that the financial toll of the investigation was the least of his concerns. Rehashing old trauma to get justice for other victims would be a huge detriment to Alec's emotional health and could threaten whatever healing he'd managed so far. Acknowledging that made it easier for Sawyer to find some grace and extend an olive branch.

He led them to the conference room he'd appointed for their use. "Marina, I can assure you we'll be extremely productive. In fact, we have a Zoom call with a victim's family member at eleven thirty this morning. Winning awards is all up to you guys." To Ricky, he said, "Keeping a sense of humor in this line of work is the hardest thing to do, but it's important. It keeps us human, and investigators who are still in touch with their humanity are better at their jobs. So, laughing is great as long as it happens at the appropriate times." Sawyer turned to Alec. "Let's take your peace offering upstairs to the break room to share with the entire precinct. Then I'll take you around for some introductions."

He looked nervous but nodded. "Do you guys need my help setting up?"

"Nope," Ricky said as he removed recording equipment from a bag. "Leave me a Boston cream so I can eat it after I pack in the rest of our gear from the vehicle." Alec set down the pastry boxes and whipped out a stack of napkins from his back pocket. He opened the top box, pulled out a glorious pastry with chocolate ganache icing, and placed it on a napkin for Ricky.

Marina sat down and removed a sleek laptop from her bag. "All of us will need to sit down later today and discuss the production schedule. The interview obviously wasn't on my calendar, so I'll need to readjust a few things before our chat." She leaned over the table and helped herself to a glazed blueberry cake donut.

Sawyer forced his gaze away from the tempting pastries to address the podcast producer. "Marina, police investigations don't work off a production schedule," Sawyer said. "I get a lead, and I follow it as far as it takes me, which often includes detours that require my attention. Things develop in real time, not according to an agenda. I know your needs are different, and I will try to accommodate them as best I can. I just need you to remember that we all want the same thing, even when we're approaching this project from different angles."

"Fair enough," Marina conceded. "I'd still like to sit down and have a conversation about the things I need from you."

"And I'm happy to do so. How about over lunch? You choose the location, and I'll treat."

Ricky jerked his head up. "Is that offer good for all of us?"

"Absolutely," Sawyer said.

"Do you want a donut before we take them upstairs?" Alec asked him.

"No, thanks. Royce made breakfast before I left the house."

Alec shrugged. "More for us." He picked up a cinnamon powdered donut and took a big bite.

Ricky sat back in his chair and waggled his brows. "I've heard all about your hottie husband. Are we going to meet him?"

Sawyer turned narrowed eyes on Alec, who coughed a cloud of cinnamon powdered sugar from his mouth. "Went down the wrong pipe," he said hoarsely. *Uh-huh.* What else had he said about Royce?

Sawyer turned back to Ricky, who grinned at him like the Cheshire cat. He wanted to say, "Not with that hopeful shimmer in your eyes," but Sawyer responded with, "It's inevitable."

"I've heard he's quite the character," Marina added. "Maybe he can join us for lunch."

"That he is," Sawyer replied. "But I'm not sure he's available today."

"I might need extra carbs if this meet and greet doesn't go well." Alec wrapped up two more donuts in a napkin and set them aside before he closed the lid and hoisted the boxes into his arms. "I'm ready to face the music."

"We won't be long," Sawyer called out as he led Alec from the room.

Once alone in the corridor, Alec cleared his throat nervously. "I want to start my apology tour with you. I acted like an absolute asshole last week." He paused as if waiting for Sawyer to contradict him, then continued talking when that didn't happen. "I've existed in this hyper state of anxiety the past few years that has continuously drawn out aspects of my persona that surprise and sometimes horrify me."

They paused at the elevator, and Sawyer pushed the call button. "Not gonna lie, Alec. I've picked up on big shifts in personality that I find troubling." The doors swished open, and they stepped inside the small enclosure. "You were so reserved during your public speaking engagements in Denver, but then you practically vibrated with energy when we met for our private discussion. And then last week was…"

"A shit show," Alec admitted. "I'm out of my depths here, Sawyer. I'm not an investigative journalist. I'm a freelance software engineer who got a phone call from a sheriff's deputy telling me that my father had suffered a heart attack at a truck stop two and a half hours north of my house. We hadn't spoken since I was thirteen years old, and I had no clue he was passing through my state. Hell, I didn't know he even had my phone number, let alone listed me as his emergency contact. The events that followed altered everything I knew about my life and thrust me into a chaotic existence I might never recover from."

Alec paused to take a deep breath. "Writing my book wasn't my way of trying to grab attention. It was my attempt at therapy, of making sense from the unimaginable. I bled all the hurt and trauma onto those pages, but I don't feel any better. He has more victims out there. The certainty thrums through my body, and I can't let it go. I won't heal until I find them."

Casting Sawyer a rueful grin, Alec said, "That nagging pulse sounds an awful lot like the drumbeats from the *Jumanji* board game, which should scare everyone. I really need investigators like you to help me see this through, and I'm sorry that my behavior didn't adequately show my appreciation. Please give me another chance to do that."

Everything Alec said rang true, and it reminded Sawyer why he'd found both the man and his story so intriguing. The elevator pinged softly, and the doors opened. "On one condition," Sawyer said as he stepped onto the first floor.

"Name it," Alec replied as he followed Sawyer.

"Do not unleash the animals from the *Jumanji* game on my city." The scene with the monkeys stealing a cop car sprang to mind.

"Deal."

CHAPTER FIVE

ROYCE HELD A DRINK CARRIER IN ONE HAND AND A FAST-FOOD bag in the other as he navigated the Suttons' uneven porch steps. In daylight, the exterior of the home looked a little scruffy, but it hadn't fallen in complete disrepair. The structure and roof were in solid shape, giving him good bones to work with. But that begged the question: Who was he doing this for? He didn't have a full understanding of Nina's prognosis and wasn't sure how long Cayden would even live in the house. Did Nina have medical debts that would exceed any profit that came from selling the home? Royce could help Cayden fix it up to turn a bigger profit, but…he was getting ahead of himself again. He breathed deeply and took several mental steps back.

Shoving the paper bag in the crook of his left elbow, Royce knocked on the door. Cayden answered with a mop in his hand and a wary expression in his icy blue gaze. His skin was so pale it was nearly translucent, and exhaustion had turned the smudges under his eyes to a deep purple. All he needed was a little glitter, and they could cast him as an extra in a *Twilight* reboot. The smell of strong chemicals wafted out of the house and made Royce's eyes water. He didn't know what

Cayden had been cleaning with, but he looked like he'd been at it since Royce left. "I think we better open some windows, buddy. I don't think those fumes are very healthy for you or your mom to inhale."

Cayden moved to let Royce enter, but he swayed on his feet and grabbed onto the doorjamb for support. Royce hoisted him back up to his feet with his free hand and kept it there until he was sure Cayden wouldn't fall over. "The house is moving, sir."

Royce assisted him to a plaid couch. "Have a seat while I open some windows. Where's your mom? I don't want to startle her or disrupt her rest."

"She's in her bedroom sleeping." He pointed to the hallway leading off the living room. "First room on the left, but I shut her door last night and haven't cleaned in there. She should be fine."

Royce set the drinks and bag of food on the coffee table. Squatting down in front of Cayden, he said, "Did you mix cleaning chemicals by chance?"

When the boy only shook his head, Royce stood back up and started opening windows in every room except Nina's. He'd isolated the source of most of the chemical smog in the bathroom. It smelled like Cayden had dumped five gallons of undiluted bleach in the small room. Royce flipped on the overhead exhaust fan and opened the small window in the shower. Once he finished the task, he backtracked to the living room and found that Cayden hadn't moved an inch in his absence. The kid stared unblinkingly into space like he'd fallen asleep with his eyes open. A disheveled swoop of black hair had fallen diagonally across one eye, but he hadn't attempted to move it. Sometimes teens went through a phase where they tried to hide their eyes under their bangs, but Cayden had always worn his hair tidy and swept back from his face during their previous encounters.

Royce sat down on the coffee table. Cayden blinked but didn't focus his eyes on him. "Do you need to go to the hospital?"

Cayden immediately sprang to attention as if someone had dumped a bucket of ice water over his head. "Hospital? Did something happen to my mom?"

"Hey," Royce said, laying a gentle hand on Cayden's shoulder. "I'm asking if you need to go to the hospital. You've breathed in a lot of fumes and seemed dazed until now."

Cayden took a deep breath and coughed. "I'm fine. Just exhausted. I don't think I've slept more than an hour at a time since Dane disappeared."

Royce couldn't just take the kid's word for it. He searched the symptoms for chlorine poisoning on his phone and asked Cay a series of questions until he felt better about his condition. The fresh air had already helped move the noxious fumes from the house. "Okay. We can skip a trip to the hospital. Let's eat some breakfast and strategize on how we're going to find Dane."

Cayden blinked a few times, and his gaze sharpened like knives. "You still believe me?"

"I do."

"And you're going to help me find him?"

"Yes I am," Royce said.

"Okay." Cayden slumped back against the couch. "Do I smell biscuits?"

It was such a teenage boy thing to ask, and it would've made Royce smile under better circumstances. "I wasn't sure what you and your mom liked to eat, so I ordered a variety of breakfast sandwiches and sides. Then I added a few orders of sausage gravy and biscuits. I also bought oatmeal and yogurt parfaits in case your mom needs to eat things that are easier on her stomach." Royce pushed the drink carrier toward him too. "I have Cokes, coffee, and an OJ to drink." When he looked back up, Cayden was staring at him like he'd suddenly grown a second head. "What?"

"Are you for real, sir?"

"I am," Royce replied. "And you don't have to address me formally right now. We're not at school, and I'm not here as your instructor. You're a family friend who needs my help."

"That doesn't feel right. I might slip up once school starts."

"Suit yourself," Royce conceded. "But let's eat some breakfast and get started."

Cayden reached for the bag and sorted through the sandwiches to find the cartons of biscuits and gravy at the bottom. "I think my mom will really appreciate this. I'm going to see if she's awake and—"

Royce stopped him with a hand on his shoulder. "You need to eat first if you're going to be any help to her. I'll need you at your best too."

Cayden took a deep breath as he set the container aside. He picked out a bacon, egg, and cheese bagel and stuck a straw through one of the Cokes. He took a sip of the drink first and sighed before he tore into the sandwich like the starved kid he was.

"I have hash browns in here too." Royce pulled one out of the bag and extended it to Cayden, who snatched it up and tore a chunk out of it. "I got apple slices too." Cayden's lips curled into a snarl as he chewed. "Or not." Royce helped himself to a sausage-and-cheese biscuit but chewed at a more leisurely pace. "Here's my plan," he said after a few minutes. "I need to meet with your mom this morning to talk about everything that's going on. Afterward, I'm going to swing by the hardware store to pick up the parts for your dishwasher. And then I'm going to the precinct to light a fire under someone's ass until they take Dane's disappearance seriously."

"And what if they don't?"

The question came from the hallway. Royce turned to find Nina Sutton standing there. She was so slight she hadn't made a single shuffling sound as she'd approached them. Dark, lank hair framed a gaunt face, but her icy blue eyes assessed him with razor-sharp focus. Nina wore pink-and-white striped pajamas, a plush pink robe, and matching fuzzy slippers. The loungewear looked brand-new, and he imagined her sons picking the ensemble out for her because it looked comfortable.

"Mom!" Cayden said, leaping to his feet. "You should be in bed."

"That's all I do. I needed a change of scenery." Nina looked at Royce and smiled weakly. "You'll do."

Royce snorted, set his food aside, and stood up. He crossed the room and offered his hand, which she took. Her bones were as delicate as fine china, and he was careful not to grip her hand too hard. "I'm Sergeant Royce Locke."

"Jason's married uncle?" Nina asked with a sigh.

"Mom," Cayden moaned. "You're in no condition to flirt."

"Ha! I'm still breathing and on the sunny side of the grave. Just let me bat my eyelashes at the pretty man."

Cayden flinched at her casual way of addressing her terminal illness, but he didn't say anything.

"Yes, ma'am," Royce said. "I'm Jason's married uncle and Cayden's instructor at the Explorer Academy."

"Don't forget handsome," Nina said.

Royce chuckled. "I think that's a matter of opinion."

She put her hands on her hips and narrowed her eyes. "Are you seriously arguing with a dying woman right now?"

Her brutal honesty took him by surprise, even though he'd already witnessed it. Royce's next breath lodged in his throat, and his words got stuck in an emotional traffic jam. Maybe it was for the best. His knee-jerk reaction was to offer platitudes that wouldn't save her life or bring Dane back. They wouldn't provide comfort as she fought a ruthless enemy that would ultimately win. Nina needed honesty, respect, and action. Royce cleared his throat. "No, ma'am."

Nina searched his eyes, possibly sizing him up to see if he was truly tough enough to take on the job. Royce must've passed muster because she nodded slowly a few times and dropped her hands to her sides. "Good. I'm going to eat breakfast while you explain how you're going to help my Dane."

"Yes, ma'am."

"I'd suggest we go eat at the kitchen table, but the room was a disaster the last time I was in there." Nina ran a trembling hand over her thin hair and looked around the room. "In fact, the entire house..." Her words trailed off as she took in her surroundings. "Is clean." She looked at Cayden with wide blue eyes. "Did you do this?"

"Yeah," he said sheepishly. "Sergeant Locke and Jason tackled the kitchen last night. I couldn't sleep after they left, so I kept going." Cayden's cheeks turned pink, and he grimaced. "I got a little carried away with the bleach. I'm lucky I didn't kill us both with the fumes."

Nina crossed the room to her son and leaned down to kiss his forehead. "What a gift you are." She straightened back up and faced Royce. "God blessed me with two incredible sons, and I know damn well Dane did not run away. My boys have never backed down from tough times."

"They're like their mother," Royce said.

She clutched her robe's lapel in a tight fist. "And that's why I'm going to stay alive until I know what happened to my son." She looked down at the drink selection. "Do you mind if I have the orange juice?"

"Of course not." He lifted the drink carrier and bag of food. "Let's head to the kitchen table to eat and talk."

Cayden swayed slightly when he stood up. Nina grabbed his forearm and guided him back down to the couch.

"Not you," she said. "You're going to stay here and finish your breakfast, and then you're going to get some sleep. I need you to be clear-eyed and strong for the coming fight."

"I'm fine, Mom." Cayden's protest was as weak as his limbs.

Nina arched a dark brow, and her son surrendered. "Fine. But I'm only taking a short nap."

Royce figured Cayden would be down for the count if he could shut his brain off after he closed his eyes. "I've got this, Cay. You can trust me and rest easy."

"Maybe it's not you I'm worried about," he said, shooting his mom a dark look.

She rolled her eyes and waved him off. "I'll be on my best behavior."

"Fine," Cayden replied. "Can I have another sandwich and a hash brown?"

Royce extended the bag to him. "Help yourself. I'm going to put all the leftovers in the refrigerator so you can tuck into them after you crash."

Cayden squinted at Royce like a gunslinger at high noon. "I'm just going to close my eyes for a few minutes. Thirty at most."

"Okay. The food will be there when you wake up."

Nina chuckled but quickly covered it with a cough.

Cayden bounced his steely gaze between his mother and Royce. "I'm not sure I like this new crime-fighting duo."

"Only one of us will do the crime fighting." Royce looked at Nina for backup. When none came, he said, "Under no circumstances will you take this matter into your own hands."

"I make no promises," Nina replied. "I am a desperate woman who is running out of time, so you better wow me."

"Understood."

They left Cayden in the living room and went to the kitchen. Either the open windows and breeze had completely pushed the over-whelming chemical smell from the house, or he'd just gotten used to it. Royce set the bag of food down, and Nina sorted through it until she found a container with biscuits and sausage gravy. She removed the lid on the gravy, closed her eyes, and inhaled deeply. Royce looked in the bag but couldn't find plastic cutlery, so he retrieved a fork from the silverware drawer.

"You really got acquainted with the kitchen last night," Nina said as she split the biscuits in half. "I can't believe I slept through it." She emptied the gravy on top of the buttery biscuits and sighed happily. "I have very few regrets in my life." She picked up the fork and pointed at her breakfast. "Except that I didn't eat this as often as I wanted to, always choosing a healthier option." Her lips twisted into a wry smile. "And I'm still dying way too young. I should've just eaten the damn biscuits and gravy."

Royce wondered if he could use that same argument with Sawyer and immediately nixed the idea. Sawyer's first husband had died from cancer in his thirties, so that remark would be absolutely cruel. And Royce knew more people died from heart disease than cancer with-out his husband throwing out irrefutable facts. But were there things he put off for a rainy day because it never seemed to be a good time? Were there simple pleasures he denied himself that he'd regret later? Did he tell Sawyer he loved him enough? Royce slammed the brakes on his rambling thoughts because this conversation wasn't about him. He could revisit all these things at a more appropriate time.

"You've gone awfully quiet," Nina said, her forkful of food frozen in front of her. "Have I upset you with my talk about dying?"

"No. I just got caught up in introspection that feels selfish at the moment." Royce took a sip of soda and added, "I find your honesty refreshing." He tilted his head to the side. "And maybe a little intimidating."

She gave him a wolfish smile before forking the biscuits and gravy into her mouth. She did a little shoulder shimmy as she chewed and immediately went in for a second bite. "Tell me your plans." She pointed at his half-eaten sandwich. "And finish your food. You're going to need your strength too."

"Yes, ma'am."

They ate in silence for several minutes while Royce contemplated how best to broach certain subjects. If he was going to help Dane, he couldn't pretend he didn't know about the escort work. Nina had already proven that she preferred blunt and honest communication over dancing around someone's feelings, even her own. Cayden had said Dane didn't like to be around his mom after spending time with clients, but Royce didn't know if it was because he felt guilty or if he didn't want her to know. "There are delicate things we need to discuss," Royce began.

Nina held up her hand to stop him. "Let me spare you the awkwardness." She kept a steady gaze on Royce's face as she continued. "I know about Dane's work as an escort. I was honest with the second police officer I spoke with, and I think that was a major reason I couldn't get him to take my claims seriously." Her voice had taken on a sharp edge, so she paused to take a deep breath. "Look, I don't think any mother would choose escort work for her kid, but Dane did what he thought was necessary to help put food on the table and keep a roof over our heads." Her lips trembled. "Not being in a better financial position to weather my illness is one of my other regrets. I could wallow in woulda coulda shoulda, but it will only waste precious time I don't have. Dane was on the dean's list at his college and working toward a finance degree when I got sick. He dropped out of school to get a full-time job at a local bank, and we were getting by until I lost my job. Dane took on additional part-time work, but it still didn't pay well enough to make up for my lost income. Cayden offered to get a job too, but his options were limited since he doesn't have a driver's license. I don't know who introduced the escort work to Dane. Maybe no one did. He's always been a resourceful person."

Nina took a sip of her juice, then closed her eyes and cycled through a few breaths. When she fixed her icy blue gaze on Royce again, he only saw determination to find her son. "He made more in his first weekend as an escort than he earned at his other two jobs in a month. And he worked way fewer hours, so he was around to help out more." Nina settled a hand over her heart. "I didn't like Dane's decision. In fact, I hated it. I wanted to cry and rage at the world, but I held that back and talked to him about being safe." Her breathing grew choppy, and Royce wondered if they should take a break. She must've read his concern in his expression because she said, "I can't afford to slow down or stop."

"Okay. But take another sip of juice."

She complied, taking a long pull from the straw. "Thank you. That just hits right." Nina set the cup down and took a deep breath. "Dane assured me he would be safe. When I pressed for details, he said that he had three rules that he always followed. He went to great lengths to protect his real identity. Dane made sure his friend knew when and where he was meeting his clients. And he never had unprotected sex. That's as much as he would say on the matter."

"It sounds like Dane had a buddy system worked out." It was more important than ever for Royce to speak to this friend.

"Dane never mentioned anyone by name," Nina said. "I know he stayed with them after meeting with his clients." She lowered her head, and her dark hair swooped forward to shield her face from Royce's view. "I think he was too ashamed to come home, but I convinced myself he liked to keep that part of his life separate." Her shoulders shook, and sniffles came from behind the curtain of hair. "But maybe Dane resented me for getting sick, and he actually ran off."

"No way," Royce said.

Nina lifted her head and met his gaze. Her eyes were red, and tears streaked down her face. "You can't know that."

"But I do. Even if he was upset with you, and I don't believe that for a second, Dane wouldn't have abandoned Cayden. No way."

"The alternative is just as unacceptable because it means he's probably dead." Nina buried her head in her hands and cried.

Royce rubbed gentle circles on her shoulder. "I'm going to get answers for you."

She lifted her head, and watery blue eyes sharpened with doubt. "How? Earlier, I asked what you were going to do if you couldn't get anyone at the precinct to take you seriously, but I didn't get an answer."

"I'll investigate his disappearance myself."

"Are you any good?"

"I am," Royce replied honestly. "And I have connections to people outside my precinct who have incredible skills."

"Such as?"

"One of my friends is an investigative journalist, one is a private investigator, and the third works for the GBI," Royce told her. Those three friends had joined forces to create an award-winning podcast and were always up to their armpits in multiple investigations, but they'd make time for him. "Social media pressure has worked wonders before." And caused a lot of chaos in others, but desperate times called for desperate measures.

Nina offered a weak smile. "Okay. I believe you'll do everything you can to bring Dane back to us, one way or another." She released a jaw-cracking yawn and wilted like a flower. "I don't think I can finish my breakfast." She grinned sheepishly at him. "I talked a big game earlier, but I think I need to rest."

"I'll get out of your hair," Royce said. Nina had only eaten half of the food, and he gestured to her leftovers. "Do you want me to save the rest for later?"

"Please." She pushed her chair back from the table, then stopped. Nina reached into her robe pocket and removed a cell phone. "Would you mind sharing your number?"

"Of course." Royce put the leftover food away before programming his contact information into her phone. Nina immediately sent him a text so he'd have her number too. "Do you want help getting settled?"

She stood up, her movements slow but steady. "No. I'll be fine."

"After I finish at the precinct, I'm going to run by the hardware store to get the parts I need for your dishwasher. I'm going to get a few wooden boards to replace the rotten ones on the porch and see what I can do about the front door sticking."

"You've done too much already," Nina protested. "I'm so glad Cayden has someone like you in his life."

"I'm just glad I can help."

Royce walked with her down the hallway and said goodbye at her bedroom door. Cayden had zonked out on the couch instead of going to his room and was lost to the world. Royce quietly let himself out and headed to his SUV. He checked his phone for messages and saw a text from Jace. His brother had sent a breaking news article that featured Holly's big arrest that morning. When Royce clicked on the link, it featured a picture of Holly wearing tactical gear as she arrested a suspect. A new message popped up from Jace, and Royce exited the article to read it.

Jace: My wife is smoking hot

Royce: Your wife is a fearless badass

Jace: I stand corrected. My wife is a smoking hot, fearless badass

Royce's brain worked as hard as the SUV's air-conditioning in the August heat. The drive to the precinct was short, so he hadn't found the perfect solution by the time he parked in the lot. Royce had worked in the major crimes unit for nearly a decade before his promotion, and he was ashamed to admit he didn't know any of the detectives from the missing persons unit very well. Royce didn't like to think of the precinct as a cliquey environment, but the units formed tight-knit families that sometimes treated the other divisions like outsiders. Holly had worked vice for several years, and many of her cases involved the other teams. She could probably recommend a detective from that squad, but she'd be tied up for hours. He'd have to settle for a referral from one of the remaining vice detectives from his old unit.

The urge to seek Sawyer out hit him hard when he walked into the precinct, but he didn't give in. Royce didn't want his husband to think he didn't trust him, and Sawyer would reach out if there was an issue. Then he recalled Nina's regrets and the questions they stirred. Making sure Sawyer knew Royce loved him above all else was the easiest thing to fix. He dropped a single heart in their text thread and hit Send without missing a beat. Sawyer immediately responded with kissy lips. Royce smiled and tucked his phone away before entering the MCU's bullpen.

"Well, well, well," Sergeant Kyomo Chen said. "Looks like we have an illustrious visitor this morning." Ky had been promoted to sergeant and had assumed Royce's leadership role when he moved over to run the academy and instruct the cadets.

Detective Shawn Ashcroft let out a whistle. "To what do we owe this honor?"

Royce rolled his eyes. "Knock it off. You both played poker at my house on Saturday night."

"Yeah, but you seldom rub elbows with us commoners at work," Ashcroft quipped.

Throwing his hands in the air, Royce pivoted back toward the door. "Fine. I'll get someone else to help me."

"Get back here," Ky said. "We're still buzzing from the sugary gifts your husband's new bestie brought into the precinct this morning."

Royce turned back around slowly. "Who is my husband's new bestie?" He couldn't have been talking about Alec Bishop. Anxiety over working with the guy had twisted Sawyer in knots and practically ruined his weekend. What had changed in a few hours? Not donuts. Bishop might win over some people with pastries, but not Sawyer.

"That Bishop guy showed up here with enough donuts for everyone in the precinct," Ashcroft said. "Even Mendoza seemed impressed by the gesture."

That irritated Royce on a level he didn't have time to explore. "I'm glad everyone is getting along." And that much was true. The last thing he wanted was for Sawyer to be miserable at work. But he didn't want him to be best friends with Alec either. "How did Kelsey react to him?"

"She was polite during their introduction, but she watched him like a hawk," Ky replied with a wry grin.

Attagirl, Kels.

"We've got your back," Ashcroft said, pointing two fingers to his eyes before turning them to the room.

"Losing my man to Alec Bishop is the least of my concerns." Once the words left his mouth, Royce realized just how true they were. "I need your help for an entirely different reason."

Ky waved him over to his desk. "Lay it on us."

Royce explained the Suttons' situation, and his friends responded sympathetically. "I need a detective from the missing persons unit who will take this on. Do either of you have a recommendation?"

"Katie O'Connell," Ashcroft said without hesitation. "She's young, eager, and recently promoted, so she's not bogged down by cynicism."

Ky nodded. "I was about to suggest her too. I've only talked to her a few times, but she makes quite an impression."

"Okay," Royce said. "Thanks, fellas."

"There might still be donuts in the break room," Ashcroft called out.

Royce waved and kept going. He did not veer into the break room to seek the donuts, even though his mouth watered at the thought. The missing persons unit was at the back of the building, walled off by glass like the major crimes, but only a quarter of the size. There were only four desks in the space, and a woman with dark hair pulled into a sleek ponytail occupied one of them. Her face was in profile to him, but that was enough for Royce to know she was a stunner. Ky's remark about her making an impression took on a whole new meaning.

The woman glanced up from a report on her desk and locked her dark eyes on Royce. "Sergeant Locke, right?"

"Yes. Are you Detective O'Connell?"

She sat taller in her chair. "I am. What can I do for you?"

"I need help with a missing person, and a few detectives recommended I talk to you." Royce gestured to the empty chair in front of her desk. "May I?"

"Of course." She shuffled things on her desk, and that's when he noticed a napkin with a half-eaten donut and several reports spread across the surface. "You're married to Sawyer Key, right?"

"I am. Do you know him?"

"We haven't met, but I'm a big fan of his work," O'Connell replied.

"He's the best." Royce gestured to the stack of reports on her desk. "Is this a bad time?"

O'Connell wrapped the donut in the napkin and threw it in the trash. "Not at all." She dusted off her hands and gave him her full attention. "How can I help you?"

"One of my Explorer cadets has a missing brother, and his family can't get the police department to take his case seriously."

She arched a dark brow. "Let me guess. 'It's not a crime for adults to voluntarily disappear.'"

"Yep."

O'Connell sighed heavily and shook her head. "Statistics don't support that logic, and I seriously doubt they ever did."

"'But our resources and manpower are limited,'" Royce recited robotically.

"Ugh. Manpower." O'Connell rolled her eyes hard enough to

strain something. "More archaic language you think we'd do away with in a department led by a woman."

"I couldn't agree more," Royce said.

"Tell me why your cadet's brother didn't walk away from his life."

As with Ky and Ashcroft, Royce told her the unvarnished truth about Dane, and like them, O'Connell reacted sympathetically as each development grew more tragic. If retelling the Suttons' story felt like twisting a knife in his heart, what must it be like to live through it? Royce couldn't take a chance that O'Connell, who was likely overworked and underpaid, would refuse to take a closer look at Dane's disappearance. "Detective O'Connell, I—"

"Call me Katie."

"All right. Katie, I know Dane Sutton didn't abandon his dying mother and his brother, who's about to become an orphan. You have no reason to trust my instincts beyond the fact I have excellent taste in men." That made her chuckle and smile. "I need someone to believe us."

"It's your lucky day, Detective Locke."

"Call me Royce."

"Okay, Royce. I'm your huckleberry."

He placed a hand over his heart. "That's one of my all-time favorite movie quotes."

"A timeless classic," Katie agreed as she pulled a notebook from her desk. She asked for Nina's and Cayden's contact information and jotted it down at the top. She looked up and said, "Tell me again what you know as fact and what you suspect is true. Don't leave out a single detail."

He fast-forwarded past the NSFW parts before Jason's visit but took his time retelling everything else as he understood it. Katie stopped him a few times to clarify things, but she mostly jotted down notes. When he finished, she put her pen down and looked at him. "I'll call Nina to take an official report and enter it into the system. I'm going to give this my all."

"Thank you."

They exchanged contact information, and Royce took his first easy breath since kissing Sawyer goodbye.

When Sal's Hardware and Home Goods came into view, Royce noted a familiar Harley in the parking lot. Not long ago, he would've kept driving, but he parked next to Eddie's motorcycle instead. Their relationship had continued to bloom since their big talk at the Keys' Memorial Day party. Eddie and Jo were frequent visitors to their house, much to Dolly's chagrin, though the Yorkie was slowly warming up to her. After spending the morning with Nina and hearing her talk about regrets, it felt like kismet that Eddie would be at the hardware store too.

Some boys bonded with their dads at a fishing hole or on a sporting field, but Sal's had been their special place. Eddie exuded rare patience inside those four walls, showing the various tools to young Royce and explaining what they were used for. He always let Royce choose candy from the selection Sal kept at the counter. Sometimes Royce ate the treat right away, but he usually stashed them until Eddie had one of his volatile episodes. Young Royce had hidden in his closet with his box of treasures and ate the candy to remind himself that his father wasn't always a monster.

Royce exhaled a deep breath as he shut off his SUV's engine. It wasn't even lunchtime, and he'd run through one emotional gauntlet after another. It would be so easy to let those old feelings of resentment and heartache taint the interaction he was about to have with his father, but Royce was tired of taking one step forward and two back. They both deserved better, so he wouldn't take his rough morning out on his dad. Eddie was at the front counter, drinking coffee and shooting the breeze with Sal when he walked in. Both men greeted him like he was Norm from *Cheers*. Instead of pouring him a mug of beer, Sal lifted the coffeepot when Royce approached.

"Want a cup? It's freshly brewed."

Royce had often wondered just how much coffee the store went through each day. The seniors who didn't meet at McDonald's or the barbershop gathered at Sal's hardware store, some of them lingering for hours. "I've had my limit," Royce said, waving him off.

Eddie set his cup down and hugged his son. "This is a pleasant surprise. Aren't you working today?"

"I'm taking a personal day to tackle some things."

Eddie assessed him with cool gray eyes. "Everything okay?"

"Things are great for me, but one of my students is really going through it right now. I'm just trying to help his family."

"I'm sorry to hear it. Is there anything I can do?" It was strange for Eddie to offer his help and even stranger for him to mean it.

"Not really, but thank you." He turned to Sal, who watched them with a smile on his face. "I'm sure you prefer this encounter to the one where Eddie and I got into an argument in your store." It had happened after Royce came out as bisexual.

Sal chuckled. "For sure. Is there anything I can help you find?"

"I need to replace a circulation pump on a dishwasher."

Sal didn't bother telling him which aisle he needed since Royce knew the store almost as well as he did. Eddie and Sal resumed their conversation when he walked away, their voices a pleasant hum that followed him through the store. Royce didn't pay attention to what they said as he compared the available pump models. But then Sal urgently called his name, and Royce immediately abandoned his search to jog toward the front of the store.

"Ed, do you want me to call an ambulance?" Sal asked anxiously.

Royce pumped his legs harder and rounded the endcap at a dead run. Eddie's cup lay on the linoleum floor with a puddle of coffee around it. His dad leaned over the counter with one hand braced against the surface and the other clutching his chest. "Christ, Eddie. What's wrong?" Royce slammed on the brakes, but not before his shoes slipped in the spilled coffee, making him plow into the counter with a loud bang. "Is it a heart attack?"

"No," Eddie wheezed. "Acid reflux."

"People mistake heart attacks for acid reflux or heartburn all the time," Sal said. "Let's be safe and call an ambulance."

"I don't need to go to the hospital," Eddie said, waving off the concern as stubbornly as ever. But then he grunted as if the pain intensified. "Well, maybe Royce can drive me."

Sal reached under the counter and pulled out a value-sized bottle of antacid tablets. "It's probably the coffee. I bought some high-octane stuff off the internet. Chew some of these and see if it helps." Sal shook several tablets into Eddie's upturned palm.

With his heart in his throat, Royce assessed his dad's vitals as best he could while Eddie crunched the antacids. His pulse was slightly elevated, but nothing too severe, and his breathing was steady. He could use emergency lights and sirens to get Eddie to the hospital fast, but he didn't have a medic riding along to render first aid if Eddie lost consciousness. "Did the antacids help?"

"A little," Eddie said, rubbing his chest. "But I think you should still take me." That settled it. Eddie was scared shitless.

And so, Royce was too. "Let's go."

"Keep me posted," Sal called after them.

"Will do," Royce replied.

Eddie settled into the vehicle, reclining the seat back a little to get more comfortable.

"Seat belt on," Royce said as he backed out of his parking spot. "And don't you dare fucking die."

Eddie chuckled, but it turned into a groan. "Don't want bad juju in your fancy SUV?"

"No, jackass. I love you, and I just started to enjoy spending time with you." Powerful emotions rose to the surface, but Royce couldn't afford to give in to them. He stopped at a red light and looked over at Eddie, who watched him with a shocked expression on his face. Yeah, Royce couldn't remember the last time he told his dad he loved him either. "And I have exciting news, but I'm not supposed to share it until the Labor Day party."

Eddie grimaced and rubbed his chest. "Maybe you should tell me now. Just in case."

"Fuck that, Eddie. You're too ornery to die." But how many people had thought that before and were proved wrong? Damn it. "I fathered a child you need to meet."

"Does Sawyer know?" Eddie asked.

Royce risked a glance and caught him smiling. "Not cool."

"Sorry. Please don't stop talking to me. It just sounded like you were making a confession, and shouldn't that be my job if I'm on my deathbed?" He patted the leather seat. "At least this is a comfortable place to take my last breath."

"Fuck that and fuck you, Eddie." But Royce's mouth quirked at the corners. "And yes, Sawyer knows. He was holding the sterile cup when I jerked off into it."

Eddie winced, but Royce knew it had nothing to do with his medical condition. "I deserved that."

"Hell yeah, you did."

"And to be really clear, I would've been uncomfortable hearing that no matter who held the sterile cup. Parents don't like to think their kids have sex."

"Fair enough," Royce said. "Kids feel the same about their parents." Eddie got an ornery gleam in his eyes, and Royce worried his dad was about to say something that no amount of therapy could cure. "Don't make me pull this car over, Eddie."

Eddie held up his hands in surrender. "Are you really going to be a daddy?" His gruff voice was soft and full of wonder.

"Sawyer and I are expecting a baby in February, thanks to our amazing friend Kelsey. We haven't told anyone else, so you have to act surprised when we make our big announcement at the Keys' Labor Day party."

"I can do that." Eddie reached over and settled an enormous hand on his shoulder. "I'm so damn proud of you."

Royce looked over at his dad and smiled. "And I'm proud of you, so you better not die."

Eddie coughed, then released a loud belch that rattled the windows and stunk up the car.

Royce waved the stench away from his face. "What the hell is that coffee made of? Napalm?"

"Feels like it," Eddie said, pressing against his sternum.

"I think that shit singed off my eyebrows."

"You're fine, pretty boy," Eddie said. "And I feel better now. I don't think I need to go to the hospital."

"Too late," Royce said as he turned into the facility's parking lot. He followed the signs for the ER and stopped outside the double doors. "Go on inside and register. I'll be in as soon as I find a parking spot."

Eddie grumbled something in response when he reached for the door.

"Don't you dare think about sneaking off. I'll tell Jo."

"Fine."

Eddie shut the door, and Royce drove off once his father entered the building. He thought about calling Sawyer as he searched for a parking spot, but Eddie's life didn't seem in peril. Royce would reach out to him after the staff evaluated Eddie instead of upsetting Sawyer over something that could be a severe case of acid reflux brought on by drinking panther piss at the hardware store. He applied the same logic to Jo. Eddie wouldn't want to upset her unless there was something to worry about. He exited the car and hurried to the ER before Eddie could escape. Royce found his dad at the registration desk, charming the pretty clerk.

The young brunette smiled and shook her head at whatever Eddie had said. "The next signature is your consent for treatment."

Eddie scrawled his name on the electronic pad and tilted his head toward Royce. "He's making me do it."

The clerk smiled. "I'm sure he has good reasons."

Luckily, they didn't have to sit in the waiting room for very long. A petite nurse with blonde hair and green eyes offered Eddie a kind smile before showing him back to an evaluation room. She ran through a series of questions as she checked his vitals.

"Your heart is beating nice and steady now," she said.

The old Eddie would've made a lecherous remark, but this new version of his father interacted appropriately with the pretty nurse.

She pulled the stethoscope from her ears after listening to his lungs. "The doctor will be in soon. She'll probably want to run tests just to make sure you didn't experience a mild heart attack. We'll try not to drag this out too long."

Two hours later, Dr. Hannah White confirmed Eddie had suffered a severe acid reflux attack, but they found other concerning issues. They suspected an ulcer had formed in his stomach and recommended additional testing. He also had a slightly inflamed gallbladder and elevated liver enzymes he couldn't ignore.

"Your symptoms and test results aren't severe enough to admit you," she said, then provided a list of symptoms that would require his immediate return. "I'm going to write prescriptions for medications that you need to start immediately, and you need to follow up with your primary care physician. I'm also referring you to a gastroenterologist, but the best thing you can do right now is to take your meds and eat very mild foods." She made some suggestions of things he should eat before laying out a long list of things he needed to stay away from. "I know it's overwhelming, but I'm going to send you home with some information that will help."

"Okay," Eddie said, sounding dejected and looking overwhelmed. "It sounds like I can't eat anything that tastes good."

"Well, Sawyer Locke will fix you right up. He knows all the best things to eat and knows tricks to make them taste better."

Eddie cocked his head to the side. "He took our last name?"

Warmth bloomed in Royce's chest as he nodded. "He still goes by Key professionally, but he's all mine in every way that matters."

"I know it's short notice, but do you think he'd mind if I came over tonight and got some tips?" Eddie asked.

"We'd love that. Bring Jo. We can eat healthy food that mostly tastes good and relax at the pool."

Eddie chuckled and shook his head. "You're not much of a salesman, son. 'Mostly tastes good' isn't a very good marketing pitch."

"Okay, fine." Royce plastered a fake smile on his face. "You'll barely notice the missing fat and calories," he said enthusiastically.

Scrubbing a hand over his face, Eddie groaned. "Don't suppose you'll take me through a fast-food drive-thru once they release me from here?"

"Sure."

Eddie perked up in the bed. "Really?"

"Most of them offer great salads, and you can add grilled chicken for extra protein. You gotta skip the rich, creamy dressings though. It's vinaigrettes from here on, pal."

"You eat like that all the time?" Eddie sounded completely disgusted by the idea.

"At least eighty-five to ninety percent of the time." Before he could ask why, Royce leaned forward and said, "We have a baby coming, remember?"

Eddie's grin stretched from ear to ear. "Yeah."

"And I need stamina for other things." Royce waggled his brows to drive home the point, but Eddie didn't seem remotely uncomfortable.

"Yeah, well, the apple doesn't fall far from the ole tree."

CHAPTER SIX

SAWYER RAISED HIS ARMS OVER HIS HEAD TO STRETCH HIS lower back. The team had worked companionably since they'd returned from dropping off the donuts. Marina went over her production timeline, which Sawyer had to admit was impressive and maybe even intimidating. Afterward, Sawyer and Alec reviewed every piece of information in Monica Horton's file. They had embarrassingly little to work with, but Alec still spotted something that made him sit ramrod straight in his chair.

"I need to show you something before we get on the Zoom call with Talia Atwood," Alec blurted out.

Sawyer checked his watch and noted that it was already eleven. "Do we have time?"

Alec leaned forward and waved his hand to get Ricky's attention. He'd been wearing noise-canceling headphones for most of the morning while he edited audio and video on his laptop. Ricky looked up with a raised brow, and Alec gestured for him to remove his headphones.

"What's up, boss?"

Before Alec could reply, the audio of whatever Ricky was working on came through the laptop speakers. Rushing wind, lively birdsong, and the musical trill of tree frogs filled the conference room. At first, Sawyer thought Ricky had been listening to an ASMR recording while working, but then Alec's voice joined the symphony of sounds coming from the speakers.

"This is the first time I've been back here in nearly thirty years," he said wistfully. "So much has changed, and I hardly recognized the place." After a pause, he added, "But I say the same thing when I look back at photographs of the little boy who used to run wild on this land."

Ricky tapped the keyboard, and the audio stopped playing. "Sorry about that. Did you need something from me?"

Sawyer raised his hand to interrupt. "Was that for the podcast?"

Alec worried his bottom lip between his teeth before answering. "Yeah. It's my attempt to record an intriguing background segment. I wanted it to come across as genuine, and I thought the nature sounds would make it a little artsy."

"Mission accomplished," Sawyer said. "This felt like it came directly from the heart instead of a script."

"Because our trip to the old homestead was a spur-of-the-moment thing," Marina said dryly, though a smile softened the edge in her voice. "I guess sometimes going off script is a good thing, but I could've done without the bugs and humidity. Maybe the next detour can take us to a nail salon for pedicures."

"Noted," Alec told her with a wink before returning his attention to Sawyer. "Do you really think I'm onto something?" His surprise and humility rang true, and it thawed Sawyer's resistance even more.

"The portion I just heard needs to be in the trailer." Sawyer looked hopefully at Alec. "Can I hear a little more?"

"Yeah, but that isn't the important thing I needed to show you before our interview with Talia."

"Just five minutes." Sawyer's whiny plea made him sound like a toddler who didn't want to go to bed.

Alec nodded at Ricky, who wore a cocky grin as he tapped a key on the laptop.

"The property is overgrown now with tall grass and weeds," Alec said in the recording. "It was heavily wooded when I lived here, but it looks like nature has mostly reclaimed this space from humans. There are no visible paths through the grass or dense trees beyond the clearing."

"And yet I have a feeling we're still going to wade into the weeds," Marina said.

"It's the only way." Alec's voice sounded distant, not so much his physical proximity, but like his thoughts had wandered off. Rustling feet through tall grass joined the birds, wind, and tree frogs. "Our trailer was over here to the right. We used to have a small shed too. The only thing still standing is the clothesline my dad built for my mother. If I closed my eyes right now, I could still feel the rasp of sun-stiffened denim against my legs." Alec's voice fell silent for several seconds, and Sawyer pictured him tilting his head back and closing his eyes. "You could've grated cheese with our bath towels," he said with a laugh. "Fabric softener cost money we didn't have because every spare cent went into building my dad's trucking business."

More rustling came through the speakers as the trio moved on from their spot. "Oh, wow," Alec said. "That dilapidated barn on the opposite side of the property is still standing. It looks remarkably the same nearly thirty years later. There might be a few more holes in the roof and more wood siding missing."

"That's a murder barn if ever I saw one," Marina said. "The entire property is a killer's paradise. You could hide an endless number of bodies out here." The shiver in her voice came through loud and clear.

"How is that old barn still standing?" Ricky asked in awe.

"Too ornery to give in to nature, I suspect," Alec replied. "My dad used to park his old red Camaro in there. He kept it covered with a tarp to protect it from the elements. I used to fold it back so I could sit inside the car and pretend to drive it. One time, I forgot to recover it, and his punishment made it hard for me to sit for a few days."

"Damn, man," Ricky said, followed by a soft pat probably on Alec's shoulder or back. "I'm sorry. You didn't deserve that."

"No kid does. And the women my dad killed sure as hell didn't deserve their fate either. It's why I can't let this go." Alec took a deep breath. "Let me show you my favorite spot as a kid, and then we'll get out of here," Alec told them. A few minutes of rustling introduced the buzz of insects to the sound mix as they thrashed their way through the tall grass.

"Here?" Marina asked with thinly veiled disgust. "I assume there's a body of water beneath the slimy green scum and floating flowers."

"They're lily pads," Alec replied. "And yes. My dad and I used to fish here. It's one of the few happy memories I have of him. He was so patient while waiting for fish to bite, but the slightest delay from me anywhere else had Andrew reaching for his belt." Alec's voice veered off again to wherever his thoughts had taken him, but the man standing next to Sawyer stiffened as if the confession made him uncomfortable.

"Thanks so much for giving me a preview," Sawyer cut in. He checked his watch and grinned at Alec. "See, plenty of time for you to show me that important detail you uncovered." But before Alec could respond, Sawyer's phone rang. He removed the device from his pocket and saw Royce's name and handsome face on the screen. "I need to take this. Maybe Ricky can cue up the big reveal while I retreat to my office for a few minutes?"

"Of course," Alec said. There wasn't a flicker of annoyance or impatience on his face, so maybe anxiety had fueled his shitty behavior the previous week.

"Hey, Ro. What's up?" Sawyer asked as he briskly exited the conference room.

"Hey, sexy. Um, there's no need to panic."

Cue the racing pulse and thoughts. "Nothing good comes from conversations that start out this way," Sawyer said.

"This story has a good ending."

"I'll be the judge of that," Sawyer quipped. "And I'll have to settle for a synopsis because I need to hop on a Zoom call soon, and there's something Alec needs to show me first."

"I just bet he does."

The growl in Royce's voice made Sawyer's blood hum in his veins, but he didn't have time for that either. "Ro, I need you to be as serious as a heart attack right now."

"Funny you should say that," Royce said. "Eddie had a health scare at the hardware store this morning. It happened when I stopped by to get parts for the Suttons' dishwasher."

"Fuck! Is he okay? Are you at the hospital? I can be there in—"

"I'm fine." Eddie's gruff voice calmed Sawyer's rising panic. "I had a horrible case of acid reflux after drinking that rocket fuel Sal called coffee."

"Eddie," Royce said. "There's a little more to the story."

"Fine. Maybe I haven't taken care of myself the way I should have all these years."

"And..." Royce prodded.

"I might have an ulcer, a bum gallbladder, and a shoddy liver," Eddie said.

"Damn," Sawyer said. "That's a lot to deal with at one time. I'm so glad it wasn't worse though."

"You and me both, kid." The older man heaved an enormous sigh. "I need your help."

"Anything," Sawyer said without hesitation. He knew how much it had cost the proud man to utter those words.

"I have all these different diet restrictions now." The hint of whine in his voice was so much like Royce's that Sawyer couldn't resist a smile. "I'm overwhelmed and don't know where to start. Royce said you would have suggestions to help. He even said you'd make a healthy dinner for Jo and me that would mostly taste good."

"Mostly taste good," Sawyer repeated, his voice hitching higher with every word.

"Eddie," Royce warned, "the acid reflux might not have killed you, but you're not out of danger yet."

Sawyer snorted. "Like I don't know how much you sneer at some of my healthy food choices. He does it right to my face, Eddie."

"I wish I could say I raised him better than that," Eddie teased. "But you're seeing proof of the shitty example I set."

Sawyer bit his lip to keep from laughing.

"And speaking of kids, I hear congratulations are in order," Eddie said.

"Damn it," Royce growled. "You promised not to repeat what I told you."

"Your husband knows you're having a baby," Eddie argued. "You told me he held the cup while—"

Sawyer nearly dropped the phone. "Whoa! Whoa! Whoa!"

"Oops," Eddie said. "Sorry."

"Christ," Royce snarled. "We gotta go. Eddie needs to find something to do with his mouth besides talking. Text me a grocery list when you have a free minute, and I'll swing by the store to pick everything up after I finish the dishwasher repair."

"Uh-huh," Sawyer said. "I might include a few choice words for you. And, Eddie…"

"Yeah?"

"You cannot ever tell my mother that we shared our good news with you before her," Sawyer said.

Eddie chuckled. "I promise to keep my mouth shut."

"I'll see you both tonight," Sawyer said before hanging up. He took a minute to process everything he learned during the brief call, and then he shook his head and returned to the conference room.

Alec was leaning over the back of Ricky's chair and squinting at the laptop. He straightened and acknowledged Sawyer with a quick nod. "I think the part I'm looking for is maybe thirty seconds ahead," he said to Ricky.

"Okay. Let's try this." Ricky made the adjustments with a mouse and hit a key.

"I relive that night in 2003 every time I close my eyes," a crying woman said.

"This is the right spot," Alec said excitedly. "Let it play."

"I should've walked with Emma to her car. I offered," the woman rushed to say, "but she told me not to worry. Em was always so independent."

Emma? Was she talking about Emma Sanderson, Andrew Bishop's first documented murder victim? Both the year and the name matched. "Sanderson?" Sawyer whispered, though he didn't know why. He wasn't interrupting a live interview.

Alec nodded and pointed at the laptop, indicating the next part was crucial. In the recording, he asked, "And you last saw her where, Tiffany?"

The woman sniffed. "At the county fair. Emma had dressed up to impress a guy she planned to meet there, but he stood her up. She learned that he'd met up with someone else instead. Em's self-esteem had taken a few blows that summer, and she was feeling especially low, so we didn't stick around. It was dark when we left, but only around ten o'clock. Maybe ten thirty. We'd driven separately and were walking to our cars when this guy approached us in the parking area. He was good-looking but older than us. Clean-cut. Dark hair. Light green eyes. Tall with an athletic build. He wore a Western-style dress shirt that a lot of men wore to those types of things. Instead of a cowboy hat, he wore a ball cap. I'm going to be honest here and say that I didn't remember what it said until an FBI agent showed me photos of Andrew Bishop nearly twenty years later. Memories of that night came flooding back. The hat he wore in the photo was red and white, but the one he wore the night at the fair was blue and white. The trucking company logo was the same. I remembered wondering about that when he told us he was a photographer."

"A photographer?" Alec asked incredulously.

"Yes," Tiffany replied. "And he said he wanted to take pictures of us. Said he'd photographed a lot of models, but we were the most beautiful women he'd ever seen. He claimed to have connections with agents who could do big things for us, and we could see a world beyond our small town." Sawyer could hear the eye roll in Tiffany's voice. "He was standing at the back of a red Camaro. It was an older one. I knew very little about cars then, but I do now after decades of marriage to a classic car lover. He's dragged me to enough shows that I can confidently say the photographer drove a seventies model. I'd bet my life on it, just as I had when I told the local cops that Emma hadn't run off with some guy who was old enough to be her dad. Anyway, he popped the trunk and beckoned us over to look at some of his portfolios. I said no way, grabbed Emma's elbow, and marched on."

"How did he act when you told him no?" Alec asked.

"He was cool with it. Called out that he'd be back the following night if we changed our minds. We reached my car first, and I offered to drive Em to her car. She'd parked farther away, and I didn't want her walking alone, especially with that guy lurking around in the dark. Emma laughed away my concerns and continued walking. 'Call me later, nerd,' she'd said." Tiffany cried softly for a few seconds before she spoke again. "Those are the last words Emma spoke to me. Her call never came, and I never saw Em again. The idiot cops said she'd been lured by the photographer's pretty promise. You know what, maybe he was right about that. Maybe she'd wanted to have some pictures taken so she could show Ryan Callahan what an idiot he'd been for choosing that skank Madison. But she never would've run away with him. And it doesn't matter if she turned around and sought him out or if he followed her and attacked. The result is the same. Your father killed my best friend."

"I'm so sorry," Alec said. "I'd give anything to go back and make this right."

"But you can't, and neither can I." Tiffany wept for a few moments before pulling herself together. "But you helped get justice for Emma, and for that, I am eternally grateful." She sniffled again. "Can I hug you?"

"Of course." Chairs scooted and clothing rustled as two people stood up and embraced. Alec gestured for Ricky to kill the audio and then turned his attention to Sawyer. "There's a single line in Monica's case file that caught my attention. An unnamed friend reported that a photographer had approached them at the county fair the night Monica disappeared. He drove a red Camaro."

Sawyer wanted to urge caution, but it was hard to do when his heart was racing a mile a minute. "That would be one hell of a coincidence," he said. "But we're going to need a lot more if we're going to connect Andrew to Monica's murder."

"Or we just need one irrefutable fact," Alec said with a wry smile.

"Why do you look like Sylvester after he just shoved Tweety Bird in his mouth?" Sawyer asked.

"Because I have an ace in the hole." Alec pulled a second laptop over and typed frantically for a few seconds. "Here. Come look."

Sawyer rounded the conference table and dropped into the seat beside Alec. On the screen was a collage of photographs taken of objects, mostly hair accessories and jewelry that had likely belonged to young women. Sawyer's blood rushed fast enough to roar in his ears. He turned his head and stared at Alec. "Is this what I think it is?"

He nodded. "I took pictures of everything inside Andrew's treasure trove before I handed it over to the FBI, and it's a damn good thing I did. They solved the straightforward cases, which were the ones that had newspaper articles or computer printouts about the victims wrapped around their trinkets." Alec tapped the screen. "These items were loose in the bottom of the box, so I figure these murders occurred before Andrew fine-tuned his process."

"Possibly," Sawyer agreed.

He catalogued several unmatched earrings, wondering if the mates had been left on his victims. There were a few charms and pendants without their necklaces or bracelets. Had those been left behind too? There was a golden tassel that had likely come from a graduation cap. Any identifying number or high school mascot or name had been removed from it, making it extremely hard to match up. There was a peachy-pink strip of velvet with an old-fashioned cameo in the center. Andrew had collected scrunchies, banana clips, headbands, and brightly colored butterfly clips.

Damn, there were a lot of treasures in that box. Did any of them belong to the same person, or did each single item belong to a different woman? If the latter were true, Andrew Bishop was likely the most prolific of all serial killers. He and Alec were on good footing, so Sawyer thought it was best to keep that thought to himself. Instead, he said, "Even if we could tie one of these to Monica, how do you plan to connect the others? How do you even know where to look?"

"The easiest places to start are the ones like this—locations where Andrew lived, both during my parents' marriage and after. I started with you because of your commitment to solving cold cases," Alec said. "Andrew kept exceptional business records for four decades. His log entries detailed everything I need to track his movements. Andrew had meticulously documented who hired him, what he hauled for them, and the destination for the shipment. He'd noted the daily hours he drove and every cent he spent on business expenses. He'd kept accordion files with receipts to back up the entries."

"You found all of that with the souvenirs from his victims?" Sawyer asked.

"No. The FBI found the business records when they served warrants on his property. The trinket box provided the just cause to get the warrants after they interrogated me for eight hours and accused me of being the killer."

Sawyer crossed his arms over his chest. "You haven't talked publicly about that before, have you?"

"Nope," Alec said. "I'm not sure I will either. If I think objectively, I can understand why they were skeptical about my accusations."

Sawyer nodded slowly as he recalled the circumstances that kicked everything off. "Son gets summoned to a hospital to see his estranged father after his heart attack. While he's in surgery, the hospital staff hands the man's belongings to the son, which includes a set of keys to the dad's semitruck. Either boredom or curiosity got the best of the son, who uses the keys to access his father's semitruck. He snoops around in the private sleep quarters and stumbles across a serial killer's treasure box."

"Plays out like a Hollywood movie, doesn't it?" Alec asked. "It was just as likely that I was bitter about the estrangement with Andrew and tried to pin my murders on him."

"Except it wasn't a script. Why aren't you bitter toward the FBI if they accused you of murder and ignored your insistence that there were likely more victims?"

"The simple answer is that I might need them again in the future," Alec replied. "Blasting them on my social media platforms won't curry any favors with them. And they could've dragged out my Freedom of Information Act request for a really long time, but they complied quickly and thoroughly once they closed the case. The photographs they took of the remaining trinkets are better than mine, and now I have copies of his trucking manifests. It's unlikely the agent assigned to Andrew's case would have been permitted to spend countless hours mapping his movements across the country, hoping to link victims to the unmatched trinkets in his box. I have the time and determination to do it, so I will."

Alec cocked his head to the side. "And it was curiosity that prompted me to drive to the truck stop and snoop around in Andrew's truck. I hadn't seen him in nineteen years. He was only a few hours away and hadn't bothered to reach out. He'd put a slip of paper in his wallet that named me as his next of kin and provided my cell phone number. That wasn't something I ever provided to him, so Andrew had sought a way to reach me but didn't. I wanted to know why."

"And did you get your answers?"

Alec shook his head. "I never spoke to Andrew. He was in surgery when I arrived at the hospital, and I never went back after I found his stash. We maintained no contact during his stint in prison before his death."

"Do you regret that?" Sawyer asked. "I'm sure you have so many questions."

Alec conceded the point with a slight nod. "But I wouldn't have trusted a word that came from his mouth. I'll let the evidence do the talking for him."

"Fair enough." Sawyer checked his watch and noticed that Ricky had been recording their conversation. Frustration flared in his gut, but he reminded himself that he'd agreed to this, and he had the final say on what got aired. "Just warn me next time."

"And ruin the take or let you hide your genuine reactions behind a professional veneer?" Ricky asked. "Never."

Alec offered a sympathetic smile. "You get used to it."

"To the recording equipment or Ricky's orneriness?" Sawyer pressed.

"Both," Alec and Ricky said in unison, then followed it up with a dual "Jinx!"

"Our call with Talia starts in eight minutes," Sawyer told them after a shared laugh. "She strikes me as someone who would arrive early, so I'm going to sign in." He pointed to Alec over his laptop. "We don't record any part of this call without permission, understood?"

Ricky gave him a two-finger salute before typing furiously on his keyboard.

Alec scooted closer so they could share a screen. Talia had already joined the call and agreed to both video and audio recording when asked.

"It's good to meet you both," Talia told them. "I'd honestly given up hope of finding out who killed Monica. We were as close as sisters growing up but had drifted apart as young ladies. She'd gone to college, and I got married and started a family. But I always loved her. I often wonder what her life would've been like if she'd lived. But now I have hope for a resolution after decades, so I thank you both for that."

"Are you familiar with my story?" Alec asked her.

"A little," Talia replied. "I honestly hadn't heard about you until Detective Sergeant Key called me last week. I listened to your audiobook over the weekend. My, you've really been through it."

"Not really," Alec said. "Andrew's victims and their families are the ones who've suffered. I want to make it right."

"Honey, you're a victim too," Talia told him. "There's no way the discovery didn't wreak havoc on your brain."

Alec chuckled uncomfortably. "That is true. I may have done a lot of research about the inner workings of a serial killer to make sure I hadn't inherited an evil gene from Andrew. I rehashed every decision and move I've ever made, looking for any signs that it might get me too."

"I don't think that's how it works," Talia said gently.

"No," Alec agreed. "I eventually arrived at that point too. I'm focused on righting the wrongs now."

"That's very admirable," Talia told Alec before turning her attention to Sawyer. "You have an impressive record of closing cold cases."

"Thank you. I'm incredibly proud of the work my unit does."

"The two of you make a good team," Talia said.

Alec bumped his shoulder against Sawyer's. "I agree."

"So, how can I help you solve Monica's murder?"

Sawyer and Alec took turns recapping what little they knew, including the newly discovered similarities to Emma Sanderson's case.

"The unnamed friend mentioned in the police report would've been Becca. Those two were inseparable. You'd never see one without the other. Becca came with Monica to all our family functions. If I'm honest, I suspected they were more than friends, but no one has ever confirmed that. Becca's maiden name was Hughes, but she's gotten married a few times. I can track her down through Facebook if you give me a day or two. I know we have friends in common."

"That would be great," Sawyer said.

"In the meantime, can I ask you about something else?" Alec asked.

Talia straightened in her chair. "Of course. Name it."

"This part makes me feel really uncomfortable when talking to a victim's family or a potential victim in this case."

"The souvenirs?" Talia asked.

"Yes," Alec replied. "If you listened to my book, you know the solved cases included trinkets that were wrapped in newspaper clippings or printouts of articles. What I didn't reveal is that there were quite a few unmatched items in the box, and I was hoping you'd know if Monica wore or carried something easily identifiable."

"I anticipated this question and discussed it with my family over the weekend," Talia said. "Monica wore the same style of clothes everyone else did during that era. She followed the same trends and shopped at the same stores. Heck, we struggled to recall what we even wore back then. But I remembered something late last night. Our grandmother had died when we were in high school, and our mothers divided important jewelry pieces among her children and grandchildren. They gave Monica a cameo broach. Do you know what that is?" Talia asked.

"Yes, ma'am," Sawyer said as recognition sparked in his brain.

"That's like a carving of a woman's face in profile, correct?" Alec kept his tone cool, but his leg bounced under the table. "It's usually set against a solid background."

"That's right," Talia said. "Monica had pinned her broach to a piece of velvet and wore hers around her neck like a choker. You guys are too young to remember that trend, but it was wildly popular for a time in the nineties. Her cameo had been carved from a concha shell and set against a coral background. I remember there being a slight chip in the shell near the bottom of the bust. The velvet choker was almost the same color as the background. They didn't find the necklace in her bedroom after she disappeared, and I believe Becca said she'd been wearing it at the fairgrounds."

"If she described Monica's outfit and accessories, it hadn't made it into the police file," Sawyer said.

Talia raised a brow. "I'm willing to bet the information in that file is thin."

"Unforgivably so," he agreed. "Would you have a picture of Monica wearing the cameo choker?"

"I'm certain of it," Talia replied. "She wore it all the time. I called my mother, who our family lovingly refers to as the archivist, and she's going to look through the photo albums from that time period. It might take her a day or two to find the right boxes and go through the albums, but she will find it."

"That's incredible news," Alec said. "Thank you. I appreciate it so much."

"You're welcome."

They chatted for a few more minutes before Talia excused herself to go back to work with a promise to be in touch soon. Alec disconnected the call, bowed his head, and sat motionless for several moments. "Holy shit," he whispered. "I was right." There wasn't an ounce of hubris in his voice, only dejection.

Sawyer looked at Ricky and Marina for guidance, but they didn't seem to know how to react in the moment either.

"Do you want to be alone?" Sawyer asked.

Alec shook his head. "I just…don't know how to feel. There's no joy in proving I was right about Andrew having more victims." He stood up and reached for his aluminum water bottle. "I think I'm going to get some fresh air."

"Me too," Ricky said.

Marina stood up. "Me three."

They all looked at Sawyer.

"I believe I promised you lunch," he said. "My favorite Mexican restaurant is within walking distance from here."

Alec shook his head. "I'm not good company right now. I, um, think I'll call it a day and go back to my rental on Tybee Island."

Marina exchanged a worried look with Ricky. "I think that's a wrap for the day," she said.

Ricky closed his laptop and began unplugging his equipment.

"You guys can leave whatever you'd like to in here," Sawyer said. "I keep everything locked tight."

Ricky shook his head. "My gear goes wherever I do."

"Understood," Sawyer said. "Guess I'll see everyone tomorrow."

The trio left much quieter than when they arrived, and the bullpen was less lively without the playful banter he'd witnessed between them all morning. The mood in the room had turned melancholy, and he'd had enough of that over the weekend. So, Sawyer continued with his lunch plans, only he had a new companion in mind. After a quick text to Kelsey, the two of them were on their way. The day had turned oppressively hot, so they'd driven to the restaurant instead of walking. Kelsey listened in rapt attention as Sawyer caught her up on what had happened with the investigation so far.

"Oh, wow," she said once he finished. "I can't imagine how Alec must be feeling right now. I'm not sure being alone is what's best for him."

"I don't know Alec well enough to say. I think I'd want to hide away and lick my wounds if I were him."

"Maybe so," Kelsey conceded.

"And I'm going to need a nickname for your husband since he has the same first name as Andrew Bishop. Does he ever go by Andy or Drew?"

"Nope," Kelsey said, popping the *P*. "You'll have to get creative."

"What do you call him?" Sawyer knew he'd set himself up as soon as the words left his mouth.

"Big Sexy."

Sawyer rolled his eyes. "Yeah, I don't think he'll care for that."

Kelsey shrugged. "Won't know until you try."

"And in other news," Sawyer said before his mind could start pondering the original story for that nickname. Big because of his height, or…

"Don't keep me hanging," Kelsey said. "What other news?"

"Eddie had a health scare this morning, and Royce told him we were having a baby." Sawyer parked the car and looked over at Kelsey. "And for reasons I'll never understand, Royce told Eddie that I held the cup during the sperm donation."

"What the hell?" Kelsey yelled before bursting into laughter. "Oh. My. God."

"Yeah, right? How does that naturally come up in conversation?"

"I don't know, but I bet you're going to find out," Kelsey said.

"Hell yeah. Royce invited Eddie to dinner without discussing it with me first. He wants me to serve Eddie healthy food that, and I quote, 'mostly tastes good' and teach him healthier ways to live."

Kelsey laughed until she cried. "Royce will be in fine form as he tries to get himself out of trouble."

"And I'll be on the receiving end of his glorious attempts." Sawyer rubbed his hands together. "And I can't wait."

CHAPTER SEVEN

STRONG FINGERS CUPPED ROYCE'S CHIN, AND A THUMB TRACED the curve of his lips as he kneeled in the shower. Hot water pounded against his back, but it was Sawyer's scorching gaze that burned him alive. "Have you learned your lesson yet?"

Royce's means of communication were limited with a dick in his mouth. Hand gestures would likely get him in more trouble, so he blinked a few times, hoping it conveyed the proper response so Sawyer would fuck his face.

"I can't remember if blinking twice means yes or no. Maybe I should remove my cock from your mouth so you can answer me properly."

Royce narrowed his eyes to object.

"Okay. Twice means yes." Sawyer smiled wryly and continued to caress Royce's jaw, his cheek, and traced the outer shell of his ear. He slid those wicked fingers into Royce's hair and fisted the strands, triggering a surge of euphoria so strong that black dots danced in his vision. Sawyer's lips curled into a snarl that was both menacing and sexy. "I'm going to fuck your face, and I will not be nice."

Don't threaten me with a good time. At least that's what Royce hoped his rapid blinking conveyed.

"Now you're too eager."

A surge of panic rose when Sawyer started to withdraw from his mouth. Royce tightened his lips around the head of Sawyer's dick and tongued his frenulum, knowing his man couldn't resist the pleasure. Sawyer's lip curled into a snarl, but he slowly thrust forward again. The thick erection gliding over his tongue made his own dick throb painfully. Royce reached between his legs to get relief, but Sawyer tugged on his hair, reminding him who was in charge. He loved when Sawyer's assertive side came out to play, such as that morning in the home gym and again when they'd arrived home early from work to prepare for guests.

Sawyer's lashes fluttered, and his eyelids drooped until only a sliver of his sexy brown eyes showed. A gorgeous shade of pink bloomed over his husband's chest and spread up his neck and cheeks. Sawyer's jaw tensed, and his fingers twitched in Royce's hair. He was resisting the urge to let go and give in to his instincts, either because he didn't want the blow job to end too soon or because he worried about hurting Royce. Fuck that. Relaxing his throat, Royce inhaled deeply again and gripped Sawyer's ass with both hands.

Sawyer sucked in a sharp breath. "Don't you—"

Royce jerked Sawyer's hips forward, taking his dick deeper.

"Fuck!" Sawyer shouted when his cock's head breached Royce's throat. He surrendered his inhibitions and fucked Royce's face without mercy, just like he'd threatened. "Christ, this mouth of yours." He cupped Royce's face with both hands, anchoring him still while he rode out his pleasure hard enough for his balls to slap Royce's chin.

Use it. Use me. And thank fuck Sawyer did, fast and hard, never easing up. Royce pulled a shaky breath into his lungs, his dick throbbing in time with the one pulsing against his tongue. Sawyer's tempo picked up as his thrusts became shorter and choppier, barely leaving the back of Royce's throat. A growl rumbled through the shower enclosure as Sawyer jerked his dick free from Royce's mouth.

"Open wide and stick out your tongue." Sawyer's command was gravelly, urgent, and utterly delicious. Royce obeyed and was rewarded with the first burst of salty essence a second later. Sawyer jerked off until his release covered Royce's tongue. "Swallow it."

Following directions had never tasted so good. He licked his lips to ensure he hadn't missed a single drop. Not trusting his lower extremities to support his weight, Royce remained kneeling at Sawyer's feet while he jerked himself off.

"Did I say you could come?" Sawyer asked haughtily.

"Try to stop me," Royce panted, working his fist faster in case Sawyer accepted his challenge.

Shaking his head, Sawyer swiped his thumb over Royce's abused lips. "You haven't learned a damn thing."

Royce's body stiffened as he shot his load onto the shower floor. He slumped forward afterward and rested his head against Sawyer's thigh. "Doesn't mean you should give up trying to teach me."

Sawyer tilted Royce's head back and traced his fingertip across his well-used mouth. "Did that *mostly taste good?*"

Royce's remark about Sawyer's cooking had seemed the least offensive of all the dumb things he'd said that morning, so he was surprised they were starting there. "I love your cooking ninety-five percent of the time. Most restaurants would kill for approval ratings that high."

Concern crept into Sawyer's expression. "I don't want my food issues to rob you of the things you enjoy."

Royce shook his head. "It was just something I said to lighten the mood for Eddie, who'd just received a pretty big wake-up call. You aren't a helicopter husband who micromanages my life and tells me what to eat. If you're guilty of anything, it's making sure I live a long, healthy life."

"We better clean up and get out of here before our company arrives." Sawyer leaned down and kissed him once more. "Though your swollen mouth is likely to give us away."

That motivated Royce to move like nothing else would. "My mouth already got a workout from running wild today. What was I thinking?"

"At which point?" Sawyer asked. "When you told your dad that I held the cup you jerked off into?"

Royce couldn't help the grin stretching across his face.

"Okay, so you have no shame there." Sawyer shook his head. "Really, Ro, how am I going to look Eddie in the eye?"

"Like you always do. Never let them see you blush."

Sawyer rolled his eyes and chuckled. "Pretty sure it's supposed to be sweat."

Royce dismissed him with a wave and reached for the shampoo. "It sounds like you have a highlight reel's worth of screwups to punish me for."

"You're not supposed to look so happy about it." Sawyer took the bottle from him and poured a generous amount into his palm. He lathered his hands and gestured for Royce to turn around, then slid his talented hands into Royce's hair and massaged his scalp.

"Lower," Royce urged.

Sawyer chuckled but didn't comply. "That will lead to other things. Our guests will be here soon, and I have a meal to prep."

"Do you want me to call Eddie and reschedule?"

"Of course not," Sawyer replied. "I just want to be consulted before you invite people over."

"You're right," Royce conceded. "I'm sorry. Eddie was this odd combination of relieved to be alive and freaked-out about what the rest of his life looked like. The dinner invite was a knee-jerk reaction."

Sawyer smacked a soapy hand against his ass, making Royce jump. "You should've called me the moment Eddie had a medical emergency."

"You already had enough stressors this morning," Royce said.

"What if his condition had been more serious?" Sawyer's question was somber and sincere.

Royce turned and cupped his face. "Baby, what would you have done? You're an incredible man, but you aren't a doctor."

"I would've assured Eddie that I'd love and care for you for the rest of our lives." Sawyer swallowed hard. "I know firsthand that dying people don't think about themselves. Eddie would've worried about his kids. He'd be miserable with guilt over all the time you'd lost."

"Eddie and I have tried this relationship thing before," Royce said cautiously.

"And we both know this time is different."

Royce took a deep breath. "Yeah, it is." He leaned forward and kissed Sawyer. "I won't make this mistake again."

"Good." Sawyer tipped Royce's head back to rinse the shampoo. "And I hope you don't mind, but I invited Alec to dinner too."

Royce opened his eyes and clocked Sawyer's smug smile. "Asshole."

"Dickhead."

Sawyer snickered as he began washing his own hair.

"Since we're coming clean, literally and figuratively," Royce said, "there's something I want to ask you."

Sawyer gripped his hips to swap their positions so he could rinse the shampoo.

"How do you feel about becoming a guardian to Cayden once his mom passes? I hope like hell Dane isn't dead, but if he is..." Royce let his words fade because they both knew what it meant. Cayden wouldn't have anyone.

Sawyer calmly finished rinsing his hair before meeting Royce's gaze. "I already called the attorney who's handling our second-parent adoption for Lil Plum. I figured she'd have some suggestions for us. If the worst-case scenario becomes a reality, we'll be ready."

Royce stared at his husband, the most gorgeous, thoughtful, and intuitive man on the planet. "I fucking love you."

Sawyer winked. "I know."

"Can I tell you something?" Eddie asked.

Royce dreaded any conversation that kicked off with that question. He turned his attention away from the marinated chicken sizzling on the grill and found Eddie staring into the house. Royce angled his body to see what had fascinated his dad, then smiled when he spotted Sawyer and Jo looking at the binder of recipes and lifestyle suggestions Sawyer had put together for Eddie. "Sure."

"I almost ended it this afternoon," Eddie said gruffly.

"Ended *it*?" Royce's heart spiked in alarm. What exactly was Eddie confessing? *Damn it!* He knew this conversation was headed nowhere good. He snapped his gaze back to his dad and caught him smiling tenderly at the pair in the kitchen. Eddie's eyes looked suspiciously wet until he forcibly looked away. *Ahhhh.* Royce knew exactly what Eddie had almost ended. "Your relationship with Jo?"

Eddie sighed hard enough to smash concrete into pebbles. He must've been hanging on to that one for a long time. "She's the best thing to happen to me in a very long time, and I nearly pushed her away because of stupid pride."

"And maybe a little fear?" Royce asked.

Eddie turned scowling eyes on his son, but his ire faded as quickly as it arrived. "That too, I suppose."

Royce cocked a brow.

"Okay, yes, I was afraid. Still am. I don't know if I can be the person she needs me to be."

Royce arched the brow higher.

"Christ," Eddie muttered before scrubbing a hand over his face. "I don't know if I can be the man I want to be." He gestured toward Sawyer and then to Royce. "Like you guys."

The compliment was a gruff, reluctant admission that warmed Royce's heart. "You don't have to be like us," Royce said. "Just be the best version of yourself."

Eddie ran a hand through his hair, leaving strands sticking up all over. He turned to Royce, a silent plea in his eyes. "What if I'm too old to make those kinds of changes?"

"It's never too late as long as there's breath in your body." Royce reached up and tidied his dad's hair, earning a grin.

"You've always been a nurturer," Eddie said. "But not me. I'm a complete bastard."

"No," Royce said, managing to keep the smile off his face. This vulnerable side of Eddie was kind of adorable, and he didn't want to discourage it. "You used to be a complete bastard who didn't care about anyone but himself. That isn't the man I see anymore."

"It isn't?"

Royce shook his head. "Pro tip number one: if you were still a complete bastard, it wouldn't bother you what Jo thought or needed."

Eddie cocked his head to the side as he considered the point. "Okay. I'll give you that one. What else do you have?"

"Pro tip number two: show this vulnerable side to Jo and reap the rewards."

Narrowing his eyes, Eddie said, "How do you figure? Jo has commented repeatedly how much she loves my strength and, um, size."

"And you think some or all of you will shrink if you let down your defenses and be honest with her?" Royce tsked and shook his head slowly. "Do you know what people find more attractive than a big, tough man?"

Eddie looked over at the house and smiled when Sawyer hugged Jo tightly.

"That!" Royce said, pointing in their direction. "A strong, big-hearted man who isn't afraid to show his affection."

His father turned steely gray eyes on him. "This is brave talk from a man whose loose lips likely sent him to the doghouse this afternoon."

"But I'm not there now, am I?" Royce waggled his brows. "Wanna know how I got back in Sawyer's good graces?"

Eddie snorted. "Pretty sure I know how, unless you got lip fillers after you dropped me off."

The damn ice pack trick hadn't worked at all. Royce had nothing to blush about, but the heat still crept up his neck, even as he shrugged. "You got it wrong, Eddie. That was my reward for being on my best behavior and apologizing for screwing up."

"This grown-up shit is a lot of work," he groused. Eddie looked toward the house and smiled bright enough to make the sun jealous. "But it's worth it when you find the right person."

"That it is, Eddie. That it is." Royce transferred the grilled chicken to a platter and tilted his head toward the house. "Ready to eat?"

"Hell yeah."

Sawyer had put together quite a feast on short notice. Dinner looked good, smelled delicious, and it would taste amazing.

Eddie tucked right in without hesitation and devoured half his plate before he said, "This food tastes incredible." He shook his head in dismay at Royce. "Your husband is an incredible cook. 'Mostly tastes good,'" he grumbled before forking another bite.

Sawyer didn't preen, but it was damn near close. "It's all in the quality of ingredients. You replace the bad stuff with flavorful herbs and spices and use healthy fats and oils. If you don't want to cook like this for yourself every night, there are companies that deliver healthy prepared meals to your door. I put some suggestions in your binder."

"How'd you get to be so smart about food?" Eddie asked.

"It has to be your mom's healthy habits," Jo said. "She's more beautiful now than she was in her thirties."

"No wonder she adores you," Sawyer replied. "I was an awkward, closeted gay kid who never fit in anywhere. I ate my emotions instead of expressing them and battled adolescent obesity as a result. My mother had friends who'd struggled with eating disorders, and she was terrified I'd develop severe problems if she remarked negatively on my weight. I eventually got it figured out, and yes, she was very helpful during my metamorphosis."

Royce coughed into his hand. "His motivation might've had something to do with the personal trainer she hired."

Jo giggled and swatted his arm.

"It's true," Sawyer agreed with a shrug. "He was a hottie."

Eddie had a good chortle over that. "Royce was right to recommend your help. I appreciate it."

"You're very welcome."

Their conversation turned to other events from the day. Sawyer couldn't say much about his investigation, but he shared what he could. Royce talked a little about Cayden, Dane, and Nina's situation, which garnered much sympathy and relief that Detective O'Connell had committed to his case. Then the topic shifted to Holly's big bust. The big press conference wouldn't happen until the following morning, but Sawyer bragged about Holly's dogged determination to get justice.

Jo set her fork down and shivered. She turned to Eddie and said, "That's so dangerous. Aren't you worried she'll get hurt or killed?"

Eddie paused with his forkful of kale salad halfway to his mouth. "I worry about her every day."

"Do you express your concern to her?" Jo pressed.

Setting his fork down, Eddie took a long drink of water. Probably trying to figure out the right words to say. Was he rolling Royce's advice through his head? Was he wondering if Jo was putting him through a test? Royce thought he detected an ornery gleam in her eyes before she blinked it away. Finally, Eddie set the glass back on the table and lifted the napkin from his lap to wipe his mouth. Who the hell was this guy? He returned the linen to his lap and fixed his gaze on Jo. "Being a cop isn't just a job to Holly. It's a calling, the same as it is for Royce and Sawyer. It's an essential part of who she is and just as important to her as being Jace's wife and Harper's mother. So, yeah, she could get killed on the job, or she could die a little death every day because our fear took something meaningful from her."

Royce stared in complete awe. It took all he had not to stand up and clap. Who was he to think Eddie needed tips from him?

"Wow." Jo fiddled with the neckline of her dress and beamed at Eddie. "That's so insightful of you. And progressive."

"Isn't it?" Royce asked, suspicion creeping into his voice now that the shock had worn off.

Eddie reached over and took her hand. "I'd love to take credit for my remark, but those are the words Holly hurled at me after I'd made a misogynistic suggestion about her getting a safer job when she announced her pregnancy."

Jo threw her head back and laughed, pressing her free hand to her chest.

"I knew those words sounded familiar," Sawyer said. "I was trying to remember what movie they came from."

Eddie lifted Jo's hand to his mouth and kissed it. "But I really listened to what she said and realized I was wrong. I sincerely mean those words now."

"Oh, Eddie," Jo said. "I love you like crazy."

He leaned forward and kissed her. "I love you too."

Royce mouthed across the table to Sawyer, "What is happening?"

His husband waggled his brows and formed a circle with his index finger and thumb on one hand. Royce kicked him under the table before he could penetrate the circle with his other index finger. "Who's ready for dessert?" Sawyer asked.

Eddie and Jo jerked apart as if they'd forgotten they weren't alone.

Jo settled back in her seat as a pretty blush bloomed across her cheeks. "Forgot myself there for a second."

"It's that Locke charm," Sawyer said.

"I can still eat dessert?" Eddie looked and sounded a little dazed. Was it from the kiss or from realizing that he could still have sweets?

"The trick to sustaining your new lifestyle is to take the things you love and make them healthier," Sawyer said. "I whipped up chocolate mousse to serve with fresh berries."

"I'm game," Eddie said.

Jo pushed back from the table. "Let me help."

Once alone, Eddie leaned toward Royce. "What other pointers do you have?"

Royce reached over and patted his shoulder. "I don't think you need my help. You've got this."

"Oh!" Jo suddenly cried out from the kitchen.

Royce and Eddie leaped to their feet, both of them looking for a threat.

"Like father, like son," Sawyer said.

Jo pointed to the sonogram hanging on the refrigerator. "Is this what I think it is?"

Sawyer smiled at her. "We're having a—"

Jo's delighted squeal drowned out the rest of Sawyer's words. "Oh my god! This calls for a hug!" She squeezed Sawyer first since he was closest, and then she ran to Royce. "When?" Before he could answer, Jo turned to Eddie. "Did you know about this?"

Eddie, fresh off a major victory, looked like a deer caught in the headlights, so Royce took pity on him.

"I just told him this morning, but I swore him to secrecy for a little while longer."

Sawyer set two bowls of mousse and berries on the table. "We planned to make an official announcement at my parents' Labor Day party."

"Oh." Jo covered her mouth for a few seconds before lowering her hand. "Evangeline doesn't know?"

"Not yet, but I might have to change that. I can't risk her finding out from anyone else." Sawyer returned to the kitchen island to grab the remaining dessert bowls.

"We won't say a word." Jo turned to Eddie. "Will we?"

"Nope. I managed to keep it from you this afternoon." He lowered his voice and added, "But we were pretty busy."

Royce grimaced but kept his mouth shut.

Jo blushed profusely and swatted his arm. "Guess we'll need to keep ourselves occupied until the Labor Day party."

The lovebirds couldn't seem to tear their eyes off one another over dessert. Royce didn't expect them to stay much longer, until Eddie scraped the bottom of his bowl and looked longingly at Jo's.

"I've never eaten mousse before," he said. "It's light and fluffy. Not too sweet."

"Would you like seconds, Eddie?" Sawyer asked.

"Could I? I mean, should I?"

"It's likely free of dairy and probably low in fat and carbs." Royce licked his spoon and set it in his empty bowl. Sawyer assessed him through narrowed eyes, looking for a hidden insult. "And delicious. Eat up."

"Okay, then," Eddie said.

Royce stood up with his bowl and collected Eddie's. "Be right back."

"Me too," Sawyer said.

Behind them, Eddie chuckled.

"What's so funny?" Jo asked.

Eddie told her about Royce's "mostly tastes good" comment, which made her laugh.

"Ouch, buddy," she said. "What time is the funeral?"

"I like you, Jo," Royce called over his shoulder. "Almost as much as my husband's cooking."

"Nice try." Sawyer took the serving spoon from his hands and heaped a generous helping into Eddie's bowl. "And yes, it's dairy-free and low in fat and carbs."

"Don't forget delicious," Royce added.

Sawyer opened his mouth to respond, but the doorbell rang. "Who could that be?"

"I'll find out," Royce said with more casualness than he felt. Unexpected guests rarely brought good news. Royce's assumption was confirmed when he found Alec standing on his front porch. His light green eyes were bloodshot, and his face was pale with a gray tinge. "I thought Sawyer discussed boundaries with you."

Alec's lips trembled for a few seconds before he could respond. "Yes, he did. And I'm sorry to show up at your door like this."

Sawyer joined Royce at the door. "Alec, what's wrong?"

"I might be in serious trouble, and I didn't know where to turn," Alec replied.

"Come in." Sawyer grabbed Royce's sleeve and tugged him to the side so Alec could enter their house. "Do you want something to drink or eat?"

"No," Alec said. "But I might need a lawyer."

"Christ," Royce muttered. The last thing he wanted to do was boot his dad and Jo out, but they shouldn't witness whatever this dipshit was about to confess. Royce headed toward the kitchen, leaving Sawyer and Alec to talk as they followed.

Eddie and Jo were rinsing the dessert bowls and loading them in the top rack of the dishwasher. "We're about to head out, and, oh—" Eddie's brow furrowed as he took in Alec's distraught appearance. "Is everything okay?"

"It's fine. Sounds like the cop shop isn't closed for the day after all," Royce told him.

Eddie dried his hands and set the towel on the counter. "Sounds like our cue to skedaddle." He and Joyce took turns hugging Royce and Sawyer, not bothering to hide their curiosity about Alec. "Walk us out?" Eddie asked.

Royce slapped his dad's shoulder and followed them to the front door. "I'm glad you guys came over for dinner. I hope we can do it again real soon."

Jo held up the binder Sawyer made. "Thank him for me, will you?"

Eddie handed Jo the keys to his car. "Can I have a minute with Royce?"

"Of course," she said. "We'll see you soon."

"Bye, Jo," Royce called.

Eddie watched her walk away and spun back around to face Royce once she was out of earshot. "Son, you have a fox in your henhouse." Eddie shook his head. "Rooster house?"

"I think it's just a coop," Royce said. But he understood his dad's message loud and clear.

"That's the podcast guy who wants to take up all of Sawyer's time, right?"

"He's the podcast guy, but I don't know about the rest."

"Why's he here, looking all aflutter and in need of smelling salts?"

Royce was speechless for a few seconds. "All aflutter? Smelling salts? What have you been watching? It's *Bridgerton*, right? Or some other period drama."

Eddie ignored him and said, "Is he into men?"

"Doesn't matter," Royce told his dad. "Sawyer loves me and would never betray our vows."

Eddie sighed and looked past him. "I know that, but I don't like the guy. He's trouble."

"You don't know him," Royce said.

"Something is off. Keep your eyes on him."

"I will, and I can start sooner once you join your lovely lady."

Eddie gave him one more hug before leaving. Royce's faith in his marriage was strong, but he still didn't like Alec in his home. He found Sawyer and the interloper sitting outside at the patio table. Alec's eyes seemed out of focus, and he'd somehow grown paler in the brief time Royce had said goodbye to Eddie and Jo. He didn't appear catatonic, but Royce worried he wasn't far from it. What the hell happened?

"This isn't good, Alec." Sawyer held a phone that wasn't his and stared at something on the screen. "What time did he leave your rental house on Thursday morning?"

"I am not my father." Alec's words came out in the barest whisper, but they packed the punch of a heavyweight champ.

"When who left?" Royce asked, though his twisting gut told him he already knew.

"I am not my father," Alec repeated, rocking back and forth in the chair.

"When who left?" Royce demanded, unable to keep the frustration and fear from his voice.

Alec flinched and blinked his surroundings into focus again. He turned pleading eyes to Sawyer first, then to Royce. "I didn't hurt him."

Sawyer turned the phone around before Royce could ask again. Dane smiled at him from the missing person post Cayden had put on all the social media platforms. Royce's heart sank with the confirmation.

"I am not my father," Alec said through gritted teeth. "I am not. I am not. I am not." Was he trying to convince himself or them? "Please help me."

As much as Royce wanted to toss him to the curb, he couldn't. Killer or not, Alec Bishop could be crucial to uncovering what had happened to Dane. "Pull yourself together and start from the beginning, Bishop," Royce commanded.

Alec tried to speak, but nothing came out. He licked his lips and tried again, and Dane's name came out in a dry rasp. Royce pushed an unopened bottle of water toward him, and Alec accepted with a hoarse, "Thanks." He drained half the bottle while Royce and Sawyer engaged in a silent communication.

Royce's gaze said "I told you so," while Sawyer's glower replied "don't start."

Alec set the bottle down, but he didn't put the lid back on it. He closed his eyes and pulled a deep breath into his lungs. His exhale was long and shaky, but he seemed steadier when he spoke. "I saw Dane at the open house, and I thought he was hot. He left before I could introduce myself, and I was so disappointed. Then Sawyer introduced me to Cory Sands, and Dane slipped to the back of my mind. At least temporarily." Alec took another drink of water, cycled through another deep breath, and picked up where he left off.

"I was anxious as hell on Wednesday night. Amped up with a mouth running unchecked. The energy pulsed through me until I felt like I was coming out of my skin. Cory was cool and very flattering, so when he offered to show me a few nightspots, I accepted. A few drinks and some conversation felt like a good way to relax, or at least try to. Cory was into me and wasn't remotely subtle about it. I wasn't feeling a spark and wanted to find a kind way to turn him down."

"How big of you," Royce said, earning a kick from Sawyer under the table. *Ouch.* "I'm sorry. Please continue."

"I'd already made enough mistakes to last a lifetime that night," Alec said. "So, I told Cory it was a bad idea for us to start anything since I was working with the police department. We'd run into each other at work, and I didn't want there to be any awkwardness. He was upset but put on a friendly face. And that's when Dane showed up. Our eyes connected across the bar, and the interest I'd felt at the precinct multiplied a thousand times. But Cory was there, and I didn't want to hurt his feelings."

"Let me guess," Sawyer said. "You excused yourself to use the bathroom and hoped Dane would follow."

"I did."

"And?" Royce prodded.

"Dane followed." Alec rubbed the back of his neck. "He said he was supposed to meet somebody there, but they'd stood him up. I figured their loss was my gain. Dane asked about the guy I was with, and I told him Cory was a colleague. We kissed, and it was like fireworks exploding in my brain. So I asked if Dane wanted to come back to my place, and he agreed. I racked my brain for a kind way to disentangle myself from Cory that wouldn't hurt his feelings, but he was already gone when I returned from the bathroom. He'd left me a note on a napkin that made me feel this tall." Alec held his thumb and forefinger an inch apart for emphasis.

"What did it say?" Sawyer asked.

"That he'd paid for the drinks and would see me around at the precinct. I double-checked with the bartender to make sure Cory had settled the tab, and then we left. Dane came back to my place and stayed there until about two in the morning. I offered to drive him home, but he said it wasn't necessary. I ordered a ride for him instead."

"Did you see him get into the car?" Royce asked.

Alec shook his head. "I walked him to the porch, and we kissed a little longer. Dane said he hoped to see me again before I left town and then headed down the driveway. The car was due to arrive within five minutes. I should've waited with him."

"At least we now have a good place to start our search," Royce said. "Can you pull up your account and look at your history to see who the driver was and confirm he picked Dane up?"

Alec straightened in his chair. "Why didn't I think of that?" A little color returned to his cheeks as he removed his phone from his pocket and tapped his screen a few times.

"Because you're not an investigator," Sawyer said. "You have good instincts but don't quite know what to do with them yet."

"Fair point." A frown formed as he scrolled. "I use their food delivery feature way too much." Royce bit back a snarly response, but only because Sawyer stepped on his foot. "Ah. Here it is. I requested the ride at two ten on Thursday morning." Alec's frown deepened into a scowl. "I only got charged for half of the quoted amount, but why?" Alec tapped the screen once more and flinched before jerking his gaze up to meet Royce's. "It's marked as a no-show."

"No-show?" Royce and Sawyer asked.

"It means the driver showed up, but the rider wasn't there." Alec stared at his phone again as if it would somehow provide additional details to explain what had happened. "But…" He looked utterly lost and sounded terrified. If this was a performance, Alec deserved a best-actor award. He sat there motionless, barely blinking. With each passing second, Alec's expression grew more blank as a catatonic fog closed in. Fuck! They couldn't afford for Alec to shut down.

"Hey!" Royce banged his fist against the table loud enough to make Sawyer jump with Alec. "Stay with me. Checking out helps no one, especially not Dane. He needs us now."

Alec nodded vigorously. "You're right."

"Does your vacation rental have external security cameras?"

"Not that I'm aware of," Alec said. "I'll consent to a search. The house, my car, my computers and equipment. Everything. I'll take a lie detector test. Whatever you need." Alec looked back and forth between them. "I am not my father. I didn't hurt Dane."

Royce held his gaze for several seconds as a war waged inside him. *I am not my father.* How many times had Royce uttered something similar over the years? And how hard had he fought to prove it? But he couldn't let his daddy issues influence his judgment, especially with so much riding on his objectivity. Royce's instincts had never failed him, and he prayed they wouldn't start.

"Please believe me," Alec urged.

"I do." But before Royce could say more, he received a series of texts from Jason.

Jaybird: 911

Jaybird: we have dane's laptop

Jaybird: we know what happened to him

Jaybird: be there in two minutes

Jaybird: this is cayden

Jaybird: jay is driving and wants you to know he isn't texting

Jaybird: he also wants to know if you're decent

Jaybird: something about the beastie boys

Royce set his phone down with a scowl. "Why do these kids send a text per thought? No capitalization. No punctuation. They think something, and they text and text." Damn, he sounded old. Once his irritation passed, the rest of the information filtered in. "Jason and Cayden have located Dane's laptop, and they found something important. They'll be here any minute."

Sawyer pushed back and stood up. "I'll meet them out front." His hand brushed over Royce's shoulders as he passed. The touch felt like comfort and praise.

"Who are Jason and Cayden?" Alec asked.

"Jason is my nephew and Dane's friend. Cayden is Dane's brother."

"The cadet," Alec said. "No wonder he's bringing the information to you."

"Dane's family had a hard time getting the police to take his disappearance seriously, so they asked me to intervene. Well, Jason had on their behalf. There is a detective investigating Dane's disappearance now, so I'm not sure why they are coming to me." Unless their method of obtaining the information was something they didn't want to tell O'Donnell. Royce barely bit back the groan when the sound of animated voices reached his ears. "Scooby and Shaggy are here." He turned in his seat to watch Jason and Cayden approach. Both guys froze when they noticed Alec sitting at the table.

"What's he doing here?" Jason asked, tightening his grip on the laptop as if he thought Alec would try to snatch it away.

Cayden pointed at Alec. "He knows what happened to my brother."

Alec held up his hands as if the younger guys were making a citizen's arrest. "I swear I don't know what happened to Dane after he left my house. That's why I'm here."

"Says the serial killer's son," Jason spat.

"Everyone, take a deep breath and settle down," Sawyer said. "We all want the same thing."

"Do we?" Jason narrowed his eyes and cocked his head to the side. "You're willing to consider this a coincidence, Uncle Ro? Andrew Bishop killed the sex workers he hired, and now his son just happened to be Dane's last client before he disappeared. Come on. You're smarter than that."

Alec recoiled like someone had struck him. "Client? I don't know what you're talking about? I didn't. We didn't." Alec swallowed hard. "I mean, *we did*, but not like that. He...I..."

"We're getting nowhere fast," Sawyer said, pushing the water bottle closer to Alec. "Take a drink and gather yourself."

Alec nodded and complied, downing the rest of the water. Royce grabbed another bottle from the minifridge under the bar. He slid it to him, and they waited as Alec drank more. He took a deep breath and tried again. "I met Dane at a bar. We hit it off, and I asked him back to my place. We hooked up, but there was no exchange of money. I ordered food, and we hung out and talked a lot. Watched a movie. And um, you know…hooked up again. I wanted him to stay the night, but he said he had to work in a few hours. I asked if I could see him again. Dane told me he had a lot of family obligations and wasn't sure he could spare the time. I offered to drive him home, but he refused. Seemed a little jumpy about it. He said he'd order a ride, but I did it for him. It felt like the gentlemanly thing to do, especially since I hoped to see him again." Wide eyes scanned the patio, searching desperately for someone to believe him.

Jason was the first to speak. "This sounds like bullshit to me."

"I believe him," Royce said.

"What?" Jason shouted. "Why?"

"Jay," Cayden said softly. "I think you're wrong about him, and Dane's messages to T prove it."

"Let's hear about the evidence you found on Dane's laptop," urged Sawyer, the ever-present voice of reason.

"And maybe we talk about how you discovered the laptop and accessed the information," Royce said, pinning Cayden with a harsh look. "Illegally obtained evidence can't be used to arrest or prosecute a suspect. You'll learn a lot more about that in the Explorer Academy."

"I told you I had a lead on where Dane might stay when he wasn't at home," Jason said. "I followed that hunch and found gold." He tapped the laptop. "I'll refer to Dane's friend as T because that's how he's listed in Dane's contacts. He wants to stay anonymous."

"But he'll do the right thing and come forward if he needs to," Cayden added hastily.

"T met us an hour ago to give us the stuff Dane had left at his house," Jason said. "Cayden figured out Dane's passwords, and we read through his WhatsApp messages."

Cayden's ears turned bright pink, and he lowered his gaze.

Royce suspected there was more to the story, but he decided to pursue the information they found instead of lingering on how they'd obtained it. He'd circle back to that later. "What did you find?"

"Dane messaged T that he'd gotten stood up by his date. They were supposed to meet at a bar, but the guy was a no-show. Dane was disappointed since he needed the money. About thirty minutes lapsed, and Dane reached out again to tell T that he's going home with that hot podcast guy who's in town. When T responded that the guy could probably afford to pay double, Dane told him that the hookup was just for him." Cayden opened the laptop and clicked on an app. "T continued to check in with Dane over the next few hours, but Dane only responded periodically. He assured T that he was safe and enjoying his night." Cayden lifted his head and stared at Alec for a few moments before continuing. "Dane said he wished the date could be the start of something real. They bantered back and forth briefly about *Pretty Woman*. T called Dane Vivian. Then Dane got silent for a few more hours. His last message came at two ten on Thursday morning. Dane told T that Edward had ordered him a car, and he'd be on his way soon."

"Who is Edward?" Royce asked.

"That's the name of Richard Gere's character in the movie," Sawyer said. "How have you not watched *Pretty Woman*?"

Shrugging, Royce said, "I saw it years ago. Probably once. Nothing blew up in it, so it's not my kind of movie."

Jason pointed at Alec and said, "Why is Dane calling him Edward if he didn't pay for sex?"

"Whether money exchanged hands is irrelevant," Royce told his nephew. "Alec has a record of the ride he ordered for Dane. His account history also shows that the driver left without a passenger."

"You didn't make sure he got in the car?" Jason asked.

"Dane wasn't a toddler," Cayden argued. "And it was after two in the morning."

"Why didn't T raise an alarm when Cayden didn't show up?" Sawyer asked.

"He assumed Dane changed his mind and stayed with Edward," Cayden said. "Something must've happened to him before the driver arrived."

"The ETA on the driver's arrival was five minutes when we kissed goodbye on my porch," Alec said. "Dane headed down the driveway, and I went back inside to take a shower. The main bedroom is at the back of the house, so I didn't see what happened."

"Five minutes," Royce whispered. It seemed like such a short amount of time, but lives could get destroyed in mere seconds. He closed his eyes and imagined the scene. Dane walking down the drive-way to wait for his ride, standing at the curb, likely looking down at his phone and not paying attention to his surroundings. An assailant could've ambushed him in the dark before he made it to the curb. Or a car could've pulled up in front of him, and he got in, thinking it was his ride. Neither scenario boded well for Dane. If they were lucky, a Ring camera in the neighborhood would've caught something. "We need to call Katie and tell her what we know."

"Who's Katie?" Alec asked.

"Katie O'Donnell is the detective investigating Dane's disappear-ance," Royce replied.

"She's going to think I did it, isn't she?" Alec folded into himself as if trying to get as small as possible. "The media outlets are going to find out, and all the good I've tried to do will be over." He shook his head and sat taller once more. "But that doesn't matter. We need to find Dane. I said I'd do anything to prove my sincerity and innocence, and I stand by that."

Royce sympathized with his situation. "I don't know Katie well, but she seems like a fair person. I'll talk to her and see if we can keep your involvement quiet for now. You are right that the media will seize on this and not let up. That won't be good for any of us."

"Unless it helps us find Dane faster," Jason suggested.

Royce shook his head. "Trust me, Jaybird. Most media outlets don't care about reporting the truth anymore, and they certainly don't care about the lives they destroy with sensationalized journalism. How long do you think it will take before they figure out Dane was an escort? How do you think they'll cover that? What about Nina? I don't want her to spend the rest of her life defending her parenting skills and getting harassed by judgy reporters."

Jason's expression fell. "You're right."

Royce found the contact he needed in his phone and dialed Katie's number. She answered on the second ring, and he said, "I have some developments in Dane Sutton's investigation."

"That's some kind of phone etiquette you have there," she replied, reminding him of past comments Sawyer had made. "But I'll allow it in this case. What do you have for me?" Royce told her everything he knew up to that point, and she whistled softly.

"Some aspects will need to be handled delicately and discreetly to avoid pure mayhem," Katie said. "And I need that laptop ASAP."

"I have it in my possession."

A rustling came through the phone as Katie moved. "Address? I'll swing by and pick it up on my way to canvass Mr. Bishop's neighborhood to see if we can find security footage."

Royce rattled off his address before they disconnected.

"Now what?" Jason asked.

"Katie will canvass the neighborhood to see if anyone witnessed something or has security footage from early Thursday morning," Royce told him.

Jason's expression turned mutinous with outrage. "We're supposed to just wait?"

"As hard as it is, you need to trust Katie to do her job. If you interfere, you might end up making it harder to find the truth." Royce paused and added, "Or get arrested." And what if Jason stumbled across the person who'd taken Dane before Katie did? The possibilities from that outcome turned Royce's blood to ice.

Jason stewed in his anger as they waited for Katie, but it didn't take long for her to redirect his energy to admiration. Sure, she was gorgeous, but Katie's unique blend of compassion for Cayden and her no-bullshit interview style with Alec seemed to impress him the most. Katie left their house with the same fierce determination she'd arrived with, and Royce knew they'd made the right call. Cayden wanted to get home to be with his mom, so he and Jason took off soon after, leaving Royce and Sawyer to deal with Alec Bishop on their own.

He wanted to be pissed, but one look at the man's thunderstruck expression melted his ire. Alec's repeated insistence that he wasn't his father replayed in his head on an endless loop. "Have you eaten, Alec?" Royce asked. It was hard to tell if Sawyer or Alec was more surprised by his question.

Alec squinted hard, as if trying to remember. "I had a donut."

"That was this morning," Sawyer said. "You haven't eaten since?"

"Uh-oh," Royce said dramatically. "Brace yourself for Sawyer's TED Talk on the evils of donuts."

"There's no nutritional value," his husband said right on cue.

Royce leaned toward Alec and mock whispered, "Just go along

with it, or he'll turn it into a Masterclass." He pushed back from the table and announced that he would make a plate for him.

"Why?" Alec asked. "You don't like me."

"Eh, the jury is still out on that one," Royce replied with a wry smile. "But I know what it's like trying to outrun a father's shadow." And he was more grateful than ever that he'd gotten a second chance to build something wonderful with Eddie.

Alec studied him for a few moments before nodding. "I could eat."

Royce headed into the house and was surprised when Sawyer followed. But then his husband pressed him against the counter, cupped his face, and kissed him fiercely. "And here I was, expecting additional retribution for my bratty donut digs."

Sawyer waggled his brows. "Oh, baby, that comes later."

CHAPTER EIGHT

Sawyer rubbed his tired eyes and willed the caffeine to kick in. Noise from the bullpen filtered into his office, and he assumed Holly or Topher had arrived, looking daisy fresh and camera ready for their press conference. Damn, had those arrests just happened the day before? But it was Alec who shuffled through his open door, looking like a zombie. Sawyer didn't know skin could look that shade of gray, but the proof swayed in front of his desk. He hadn't expected to see Alec again so soon after dropping him off at the hotel he'd booked until the SPD released his rental house.

"Sit down before you collapse," Sawyer demanded. "What are you doing here?"

Alec dropped into the office chair and closed his eyes. "I have to do something productive, or I'll go out of my mind."

"Have you slept?"

Alec shrugged. "Here and there?" He opened his bloodshot eyes. "What about you?"

"Same."

More bustling came from the bullpen, and Sawyer caught snatches of conversation between Alec's team. Marina carried a takeout bag and a drink carrier. She met Sawyer's gaze and nodded toward the conference room.

"Your cavalry and carbohydrates are here," he said.

Alec must've drifted to sleep because he jerked upright, wide eyes darting around the room. "What?"

"I don't think you're going to be much help in this condition," Sawyer said. "I hope you didn't drive here."

Alec shook his head. "Not until your guys finish searching my car. Marina and Ricky are staying at the same hotel. They dropped me off at the door before they went to get breakfast."

"And you practically arrived down here at the same time?" Sawyer pressed.

Alec's shoulders rose and fell dramatically with a deep sigh. "I waited upstairs, hoping to run into Cory so I could apologize for my shitty behavior Wednesday night. But no such luck."

Sawyer sympathized, he truly did, but Alec was in no condition to help anyone, least of all himself. "Look, I get the impression that Cory only would've been happy with one outcome that night. He realized it wouldn't happen and bailed instead of talking to you like an adult. What part of that is your fault?"

"Maybe, but I could've—"

"Had sex with him to spare his feelings and really send the wrong signal?" Sawyer asked.

Alec slumped back in the chair. "Yeah, okay. I still could've handled the situation better." He briefly closed his eyes and inhaled a shaky breath. "I really connected with Dane. I mean…I can't remember a time when someone didn't ask about Andrew. He didn't care about my notoriety. And it felt like he was having a good time too, and I instinctively knew that was a rare and precious thing for him. Our conversations didn't get too deep, so I didn't know what was going on in his life. He deserves better." Alec met his gaze. "I can't allow myself to think he's dead. I wish there was something more I could do to help."

Sawyer's cell phone rang before he could respond. He didn't recognize the number and considered letting it go to voicemail and then decided against it. "Head on in and get some breakfast. It might help." Alec slowly stood as Sawyer accepted the call. "Detective Sergeant Key," he said.

"Good morning, it's Talia Atwood calling. I have some great news."

Sawyer snapped his fingers to get Alec's attention and pointed at his phone. "Good morning, Talia. It's good to hear from you."

"You'll really think so when you know why I'm calling."

"Speakerphone," Alec whispered before hurrying out the door in a sudden burst of energy. He returned quickly with a recording device in his hand.

Ahhh. That's what sparked the man back to life. "Alec is here with me. Would it be okay if I put you on speakerphone so we can record the conversation?"

"Of course," she said.

Sawyer tapped his phone, and Alec pressed Record. "Now we're all set. What do you have for us, Talia?"

"I tracked Becca down through Facebook, and we talked at length last night. Remember, she's the one who mentioned the photographer to the police officer."

"Yes," Sawyer and Alec said.

"Obviously, Becca was curious about why I was reaching out after all these years. I tried not to overstep, but I told her about our conversation. I worried she wouldn't talk to you otherwise. Becca struggled for so long after Monica disappeared."

"It's okay," Alec said. "It's impossible to keep an investigation like this a secret for long."

"I'm fine with it too," Sawyer added.

"Oh, good," Talia sighed. "Becca agreed to speak to you both and gave me her contact information."

"Could you please email it to me?" Sawyer asked.

"Of course. I have more good news. My mother came through like I knew she would. She found photographs of Monica wearing her cameo choker. I will overnight those to you, but in the meantime, I've scanned them into my computer this morning and will add them to the email. The photos are thirty years old and not the best quality to begin with, so my scans aren't great."

"It's a place to start though, Talia. Thank you so much," Sawyer said.

"You're welcome. Sending it through now. Will you keep me posted with any updates?"

"Absolutely. Have a good day."

"You too. Bye now," she said before disconnecting the call.

Sawyer pulled up his email on his desktop and clicked on the images at the bottom. Alec rounded his desk and peered over his shoulder. "These are pretty fuzzy." And it only got worse when Sawyer tried to zoom in on the choker.

"Do you have anyone on staff who can enhance the photos?" Alec asked. "And perhaps make the images sharper?"

Sawyer grimaced. "We do."

Alec stopped the recording. "Cory?"

"Uh-huh. I can do this by myself if you think it will be too awkward," Sawyer offered.

"No. This is too important, so I need to set everything else aside."

Sawyer hoped the forensic analyst felt the same way. He looked up Cory's extension in the directory and dialed. "Here goes."

Cory answered just before the call transferred to voicemail. If he hadn't identified himself, Sawyer wouldn't have recognized his voice. The guy who answered was a hollowed husk of the vivacious person Sawyer knew. "Oh, hi," Cory said when he realized who'd called. His attempt at perkiness fell flat, and Alec cringed. "What can I do for you?"

"We are hoping you could enhance some photos for us to make the images clearer," Sawyer said.

"We?" Cory asked dryly. "Is this for the project with *him*? Am I on speakerphone?"

"You are," Sawyer said. "But we're not recording."

"Is *he* there?"

"I am," Alec said. "I know you're upset with me, and rightfully so, but I hope that won't stop you from helping us close an investigation."

"Will you include me in the podcast?" Cory asked.

"We'd like to, but only if that's something you want," Alec said. "We can keep your contribution anonymous if that's your preference."

Cory snorted. "I might as well get something out of meeting you."

"Ouch," Sawyer mouthed as he rubbed his chest.

Alec dismissed his taunting with an eye roll. "Should we come there? It would be Sawyer, the videographer, and me."

"Sounds like it will be easier if I come to you," Cory said. "I'll be there in a few minutes."

His arrival took more like twenty minutes, and Sawyer understood why when Cory came through the door. If Sawyer hadn't known to look for him, he might not have recognized the young guy. His sandy-brown hair looked slicked back, maybe wet even, but the differences didn't stop there. Cory wore his typical work outfit of khaki pants and an SPD polo shirt, but he seemed…edgier, maybe? Sawyer tried hard not to stare as he looked for the specific differences besides his hairstyle. His pants fit differently. Perhaps they were a slim fit instead of a relaxed cargo style. Cory wore a leather cuff bracelet embellished with stamped letters and metal accents. It seemed vaguely familiar to Sawyer, so he must've seen him wearing it before, even though it felt out of place. The biggest difference was the flat, sharklike expression in his honey-brown eyes. Where had his sparkle gone? Had one disappointing night out really set him back this far? He must be going through something else.

"I'm ready," Cory said, keeping his dull gaze locked on Sawyer. "Where are the photographs?"

"Let's go into the conference room so we can document the interaction," Alec said with mock cheerfulness.

Sawyer led the way, thinking Cory would be right on his heels, but Alec asked him to hang back for a minute.

"Can I take you to lunch so I can apologize properly?" Alec asked, his voice heavy with regret.

Sawyer slowed his gait so he could eavesdrop, and his effort paid off.

"No," Cory said flippantly. "Today doesn't work for me. Maybe tomorrow."

"Okay, yeah. Just let me know when and where."

Cory hummed noncommittally and followed Sawyer, who hurried into the conference room so he wouldn't get caught. Marina looked up from her task and raised a brow.

"We've asked Cory to come down from forensics to see if he can enhance the photographs Monica's cousin sent us," Sawyer said.

Marina and Ricky exchanged a knowing glance before turning their rapt attention to the door behind him. Sawyer didn't know how much Alec had told them, but they at least knew about Cory.

"Make yourself comfortable," Sawyer told him, gesturing to the long table. He introduced Marina and Ricky to Cory and explained their roles in the project. "Ricky is going to record this for the podcast, right?"

"Yes!" Ricky snapped his fingers. "I got my equipment right here." He hoisted a small video camera, made a few corrections, and gestured for them to resume their conversation.

Cory took a seat at the far end of the table and opened his laptop. "Did I hear you say that I'm enhancing emailed photos?"

"That's correct," Sawyer said. "She scanned the images and emailed them to me."

"Not ideal," Cory said as he typed furiously on his keyboard. "Scanning often makes the resolution worse because people don't realize they can change their settings." He looked up and offered Sawyer his first genuine smile. "But I am very good at what I do."

"Talia is overnighting the originals from Jacksonville," Alec interjected as he sat opposite Cory. "You can work with those when we get them."

Sawyer noted the slight tensing in Cory's shoulders, but he otherwise treated Alec as the invisible man, keeping his gaze locked on Sawyer.

"Send me what you have." Cory rattled off his email address, and Sawyer started typing.

"We'll need to cut that part out," Alec said. "He won't want a bunch of randos spamming him with email."

Cory jerked his head up and acknowledged Alec for the first time. "Worried they'll accept my invitation to go out and then blow me off too?"

Oh boy. "Images sent," Sawyer said, hoping to steer the conversation back on track.

"Got them," Cory replied. "Hmmmm. These aren't half-bad. What are you looking for?"

"We would like a clearer image of the choker the petite blonde is wearing in all these photos," Sawyer said. "There are characteristics on the cameo that we are hoping to match to the choker in the FBI evidence photographs."

Cory looked at Alec again, but the derision from earlier had vanished. "You think this cameo is part of your father's unmatched souvenirs?" Clearly, Alec had discussed the case with Cory last week, and Sawyer was concerned about what else he knew.

"I'm almost positive," Alec replied. "Can you help us?"

Cory studied the photos and clicked around on his keyboard. "You're talking about two different applications to clear up the images and get a closer look at the cameo, but I'll give it my all."

"Do you mind if Ricky stands behind you to get a better look at what you're doing?" Alec asked.

"Not at all."

Sawyer moved over so Ricky could have a good view. Cody explained the process of cleaning up the images and then showed each new version in a split screen to compare it to the original. Sawyer tuned out the conversation and just watched the image become clearer in stages. Cody saved his progress when he was happy with the results and switched to zooming in on the choker. The process seemed to take forever but was quite fascinating. Alec remained seated across the table and let Ricky handle the interview until Cory sat back in his chair and announced he'd done as much as he could with the scanned photos.

Sawyer stared at the image on the screen in complete awe. "That's amazing. Can you send all the final images to me?"

"Of course." Cody's fingers flew across the keyboard. "Done."

Alec stood up, rounded the table, and then froze when he saw the image displayed on the screen. He stared at it for a long time before turning to meet Sawyer's gaze. "Seems like a conversation with the FBI is in order."

"Absolutely," Sawyer said. "Thank you so much, Cory. I think you've helped us blow the case wide open."

The forensic tech closed his laptop and stood up. Excitement sparkled in his eyes again as he looked from Sawyer to Alec. "Really?"

"You've absolutely proved to me that my dad killed Monica Horton," Alec said. "Now I just need to convince the FBI."

"Cory, we need you to keep this quiet," Sawyer cautioned. "We don't want a media frenzy to descend on us before we're ready to go public with our findings."

The warning seemed to snuff the joy right out of Cory, and the life in his eyes switched off again. "I know my professional responsibilities," he replied dryly. "I never discuss my work." Cory closed his laptop and faced them. "If you'll excuse me, I need to head back upstairs to work on other things before lunch."

The team thanked Cory profusely as he left, but he didn't acknowledge them.

"You dodged a bullet there," Marina said.

"Yeah," Ricky agreed, the trademark twinkle in his eyes shining brighter than usual. "That wasn't nearly as dramatic as I thought it would be."

"Oh, hush," Alec told them as he moved to his own laptop. "Can you send those photos to me? I want to compare Cory's enhanced image to the evidence photos."

Sawyer forwarded them to Alec and waited for him to display them side by side. "Holy shit."

"See that shadow on the cameo in the enhanced photo? It's in the same place as the chip on the cameo I found in Andrew's box."

It felt irrefutable to Sawyer. "Add in Becca's account of the photographer with the red Camaro, and I think the FBI has to take this claim seriously."

"And I have a good picture of Andrew with his hot rod," Alec said. "I haven't shared it publicly because I'm saving it to use as the podcast cover art and possibly a second book cover. I wonder if Becca would do a photo lineup for us."

"It's a good idea, but I think that's something the FBI should decide."

"And if they don't?" Alec pushed.

"We talk to Chief Mendoza and see how he wants us to proceed. We could close Monica's case as solved without the FBI's involvement. I know that won't be as newsworthy, but I think Monica's family would appreciate the closure."

Alec pulled up the contacts in his phone. Glancing over at Ricky, he said, "Are you still recording?"

"Hell yeah. This is documentary gold."

Alec dialed a number, and they listened as it rang. The call went to a voicemail box where a woman identified herself as Special Agent Veronica Wilson. She wasn't available to talk and asked the caller to leave a message and their contact information. Alec calmly introduced himself, gave a brief recap of what they'd discovered, and left his phone number. "Now, we wait."

A knock sounded on the doorjamb, and they all turned to see Detective O'Connell standing just outside the conference room. She wore a somber expression, and Sawyer braced for bad news.

"Can I have a word?" O'Connell asked Alec.

"Sure."

"You can use my office," Sawyer said.

"Can Sawyer come too?" Alec asked the detective.

She shrugged and stepped back. "It's fine by me."

Sawyer followed them into his office and shut the door. He opted to stand off to the side and gestured for O'Connell to take his chair.

"Thanks," she said. "I just wanted to give you a brief update on where I'm at. We completed the search of your car and your house, so I wanted to return these to you." She placed a set of keys on the desk in front of Alec. "I do not consider you a suspect. Besides your full cooperation in the matter, I have located footage from multiple Ring cameras in your neighborhood that back up your statement. The neighbor directly across the street really needs to adjust their motion settings. They captured the shared kiss on the porch, Dane walking down the driveway, and you going inside the house."

Alec bolted upright. "What else did it show?"

"Two cars stopping in front of your house," O'Connell replied. "The first was a four-door silver sedan. We found the vehicle on additional footage in the neighborhood and know it was parked down the street for a significant period, as if watching your house."

Alec jerked like she'd slapped him.

"I can tell from the time stamps from both cameras that the car pulled away from the curb as soon as Dane stopped at the end of your driveway. He was busy on his phone and got into the back seat of the silver sedan without checking to see if the car was his ride. His Lyft driver arrived two minutes later in a small black SUV."

"I didn't tell him what kind of car to expect," Alec said.

"This isn't your fault," Sawyer reminded him. "What else did the cameras catch?"

"A device at the end of the street came on when a cat ran across the lawn, and it captured the silver sedan turning left to exit the neighborhood. Some of the license plate lights were out, so I only have a partial number, but it will be enough to get a match. I've got someone scouring the DMV database right now."

"That's certainly helpful," Sawyer said.

"I'm waiting on cell phone tower information so we can check the pings from Dane's phone. I've prepared a warrant for his phone records, and I'm waiting for a judge's signature. We could find other important clues in that data. We're going to figure out what happened to Dane."

"I appreciate you sharing this information with me, Detective O'Connell," Alec said. "Savannah is lucky to have someone like you."

"That's nice of you to say. I'll let you know when I have more updates."

Alec looked incapable of speaking, so he nodded.

After she left, Ricky and Marina joined them. It was obvious Alec had told his team about meeting Dane too.

"Did she have good news?" Marina asked.

"She has a few leads," Sawyer told them.

"That's something positive," Ricky said.

Alec tilted his head back against the wall and closed his eyes. Then he yawned wide enough to make his jaw crack.

"Gross," Ricky grumbled.

"You look like a gentle breeze could knock you over," Marina added. "Let's go get something to eat for lunch, and then I'll drop you back at the hotel. You've done as much as you can today. It's time to rest."

"Detective O'Connell returned the keys to his house and car," Sawyer told them.

"We can check you out of the hotel and take you back to the beach house. How's that sound?"

"Okay," Alec replied.

Sawyer wondered if he'd need help to stand, but then Alec pulled himself together after another jaw-cracking yawn. He flopped down in his desk chair after the trio left, closing his eyes and hoping for just a few minutes of peace. His ringing cell phone shattered his hopes almost immediately. Sawyer cracked open one eye to see the caller ID, then smiled when he saw the picture of him and Evangeline on his wedding day. It wasn't unusual for her to reach out with a spontaneous lunch invitation, so Sawyer injected a smile into his voice when he accepted the call.

"Hello, son." Evangeline's voice was low, almost menacing. "Is there something you forgot to tell me?"

"Um…" Sawyer sluggishly searched his brain for an oversight but couldn't come up with anything.

"Think carefully. Is there a major life event you've planned behind my back?"

Awareness kicked him in the balls. His mother knew about their Lil Plum. But how? Eddie wouldn't have told her. Soft yipping came through the phone. Dolly! Evangeline loved to spoil the fur grandkids and had probably swung by to let Dolly outside or deliver goodies. He'd told Royce it was a bad idea to hang that sonogram on the refrigerator, but once it was there, neither of them could take it down and put it in a drawer.

"Well—" That was as far as Sawyer got before a shrill squeal cut him off. He pulled his phone away until the ringing in his ears subsided.

"Sorry," Evangeline said a few moments later. "You were saying."

"Kelsey is helping Royce and me with a very special project. We were planning to surprise everyone at your Labor Day party."

"Hang on, please," Evangeline said, then set her phone down on a surface. "Yes! Whew! It's about time! You're going to have a brother or sister, Bonesy and Doll Doll." His mother whooped and hollered for a few minutes while his heart swelled with love. Evangeline cleared her throat, reclaimed her phone, and calmly said, "Sawyer, I am thrilled for you and Royce. I cannot wait to celebrate this with you."

"Really, I couldn't tell."

"Oh, hush," Evangeline said. "I've been planning this moment since the day I met Royce Locke. I have so many questions." She proceeded to fire them at him. "How's my sweet girl Kelsey? When's her due date? Are you going to find out the baby's gender? Have you picked out names? Oh! Oh! What about a nursery theme?"

Sawyer was debating how much he wanted to reveal when Alec reappeared in his doorway, looking wild-eyed and frantic. "Mom! Something came up at work that needs my immediate attention. I need to go. I love you and will call you later." He disconnected the call before she could respond and stood up. "What's wrong?"

Marina and Ricky ran into the bullpen, winded and worried.

"Fuck, Sawyer," Alec said. "I know who took Dane!"

Sawyer's heart slammed against his ribs. "Who?"

Alec clutched his chest and slumped against the doorway as if that burst of energy could be his last. "Cory," he husked.

"What's he talking about?" Sawyer asked Marina and Ricky.

"We ran into that forensics guy on the way to the parking lot," Ricky said. "He and Alec walked ahead of us, so I didn't hear what they said. Did you, Mar?"

"Cory said something about going home for an early lunch," she replied. "Guess he lives close by. Everything was fine until Cory reached out and placed his hand on Alec's forearm."

"It was Dane's," Alec huffed.

"Dane's what?" Sawyer pressed.

"The leather cuff bracelet Cory had on belonged to Dane. I admired it when he was at my house. Dane told me it had been a gift from his brother. I didn't notice Cory wearing it earlier, but I was too focused on the investigation."

Sawyer grabbed his phone and checked the post Cayden had shared about his missing brother. Sure enough, Dane wore a leather cuff like the one Cory had been wearing.

"Seven-two-one-nine," Alec husked. "Seven-two-one-nine."

"What the hell?" Marina asked.

"He's malfunctioning," Ricky suggested.

But Sawyer knew exactly what those numbers meant.

Alec straightened to his full height and waved them off. "Silver sedan. Four doors. Partial license plate is seven-two-one-nine. Cory just drove off in the car that Dane got into in front of my house."

Holy shit. "I'm calling Detective O'Connell."

CHAPTER NINE

"**W**ANT TO HEAD OUT AND GRAB A BITE TO EAT BEFORE THE cadets arrive?" Tara asked.

Their students spent the first half of their day at their respective high schools and the second half at the Explorer Academy, so lunchtime was the sacred calm before the storm.

Royce looked up from scanning his syllabus again after making mild adjustments to his curriculum. "I'm always ready to eat. Just give me a second to save this final draft."

Tara snorted. "Final draft? You've been saying that for the last month."

Royce had expanded the lessons on illegal searches and seizures after the previous night's events, though he only planned to review the training sessions and behavior expectations with the cadets on their first day of school. He'd be sure to make eye contact with Cayden during those highlights. "Well, recent events have required me to spend extra time in certain areas." He pushed back from his desk once his progress was saved. "What sounds good for lunch?" His phone rang, and he saw it was Katie calling him, hopefully with an update on Dane's case. "Hang on. I have to take this," Royce told Tara before answering. "What's the word, Katie?"

"Alec just cracked Dane's case wide open. I'm going to approach the suspect and need some backup. Are you free?"

"I am now, but my students are due to arrive in an hour," Royce said.

Sensing the urgency, Tara shooed him and mouthed, "I've got this."

"But my partner's got it covered, so I'm heading upstairs now."

"Meet me in the parking lot," Katie said before disconnecting.

"Thanks, Tara," Royce called over his shoulder as he bolted from the room. He skipped the elevator and took the stairs two at a time, getting the cardio he'd skipped to linger in bed that morning. Royce earned some raised brows as he hustled through the precinct and burst out the back doors.

Katie waited for him at the curb, and he climbed inside her Charger. She gunned the engine as soon as he shut the door and turned on the lights and sirens to merge into traffic. He got a text from Sawyer and couldn't believe what it said.

"Cory Sands took Dane? The guy from forensics?" Royce asked.

Katie told Royce everything she'd gleaned from the video and then explained how Alec had put all the pieces together.

"Cory?" Royce repeated. "I get what you're saying. He has a major crush on Alec and got jealous when their night didn't go as planned. But to kidnap the guy he'd taken home instead is…"

"Something an unhinged fan with obsessive tendencies might do," Katie replied. "Maybe the car similarities and the matching partial plate number are just a big coincidence, but I don't think so."

"Do you really think Cory went home for lunch like he told Alec?"

"Probably," Katie said. "Cory has no reason to believe we're onto him, and I think he's sticking close to home because he has a situation he's not equipped to handle."

Royce jerked his head in her direction. "You think Dane is alive?"

"That's my hope," Katie replied. "Cory could have acted on impulse and then panicked, unsure what to do with Dane. He likely has severe mental health issues, but that doesn't make him a killer." She sighed and glanced at Royce. "Or he just hasn't worked up his courage to kill him yet."

"Shit."

Katie killed the lights and sirens a few blocks from Cory's house so they wouldn't announce their arrival prematurely. She parked two doors down, and they casually walked the short distance to avoid drawing attention. The silver sedan from the video footage was in front of a tidy bungalow with a meticulous lawn. They made brief eye contact before Katie pounded on the front door.

"Cory Sands! It's the Savannah Police Department. Open up."

Sounds of movement came from the other side of the door, getting louder as someone approached. Royce's palm rested on the butt of his gun, and he really hoped he wouldn't have to use it. He prayed Katie was right about Dane still being alive because he'd never wanted to be more wrong about something.

The door opened a few inches to reveal a sliver of Cory's face, but it was enough for Royce to know something was very off. The only visible honey-brown eye darted between Royce and Katie without recognition or expression. No curiosity about why the SPD had forcefully knocked on his door, and he didn't express any irritation that they'd interrupted his lunch. Just complete emptiness. Without a warrant, they couldn't force their way inside and would need to rely on other methods to get his cooperation. Since Katie was the lead detective, Royce let her set the tone.

"Open the door so I can fully see you and your hands," Katie commanded.

"What's this about?" Cory asked, his voice as bland as his gaze was vacant. "Why are you here?"

"Open the door. Now. I need to see your hands."

Cory's eye dropped lower to where her hand rested on the butt of her weapon before snapping back up to her face. He blinked, and Royce thought he saw a spark of something in his eyes, maybe a hint of fear, but it fizzled out. Cory eased the door open until his body came into full view. His weapon-free hands fell to his sides, where his thumbs fidgeted with the seams in his pant legs. "Now, will you tell me why you're here?" Annoyance had crept into his tone.

"What the hell have you done with Dane Sutton?" Katie demanded. Oh damn. She went straight in. "And don't bullshit me," she added before a lie could form on Cory's mouth. "Security cameras captured you picking Dane up in front of Alec Bishop's house. No one had seen or heard from him since."

"You're lying," Cory said with the least amount of conviction Royce had ever heard from a suspect. He shook his head in further denial. But whose benefit was that for? His or theirs?

A dull scraping sound came from inside the house. It sounded like wood scraping against wood. It happened again but louder the second time.

Hope flared in Royce's heart. "Who's in there with you?"

"No one," Cory said, then ruined the denial when he glanced over his shoulder.

"Mind if we come in?" Katie asked.

"Do you have a warrant?" The smug bastard knew they didn't, or they would've presented it already.

A soft thud came from inside the house, followed by more scraping and then rhythmic thumping. Royce's pulse kicked up a notch because it sounded like someone in distress was trying to get their attention. The series of noises repeated. *Thud. Scrape. Thump. Thump. Thump. Thump.* Royce shifted closer to the door to see deeper into the house and, in doing so, encountered a foul smell that went beyond ordinary untidiness. It smelled of human excrement and body odor, but thankfully, not decomposition. *Thud. Scrape. Thump. Thump. Crack. Crash.*

Katie and Royce reacted immediately. She grabbed Cory's arm, yanked him forward, and subdued him on the porch while Royce drew his gun and rushed inside the house.

"Hey!" Cory screamed. "You don't have a warrant."

"We don't need one when there's evidence of a violent crime in progress," Katie said.

"Dane Sutton!" Royce called. "It's Sergeant Locke with the Savannah Police Department! You're going to be okay, buddy." Royce's gun led the way, sweeping left and right as he navigated the house, clearing each room as he went. The living room had been turned into a temporary bedroom with pillows and blankets strewn across the sofa. Clothes were piled high in a chair and littered the floor. The kitchen and dining nook were just as cluttered with dishes overflowing the sink, spilling onto the countertops with takeout cartons and pizza box castoffs. There were only three wooden chairs around the matching oak table tucked into the corner of the kitchen nook, and Royce knew where he'd find the fourth. The stench grew worse toward the back of the house, where the bedrooms and bathroom would be. "Dane! Can you hear me?"

A muffled, hoarse cry came from the last room on the right. Royce repressed the urge to run straight there and cautiously cleared an empty bedroom and the bathroom first before moving farther down the hallway. They didn't know if Cory had an accomplice or what methods had been used to restrain Dane. Royce didn't want to stumble into a situation that would get anyone killed. With his heart in his throat, Royce eased closer to the doorway, his gun aimed steadily in front of him. He paused momentarily, listening for signs of a threat, but only heard muffled moans. Royce swept into the room, clearing each corner, the bathroom, and the closet before holstering his gun and dropping to his knees beside Dane's bound body. He'd been tied to the missing wooden chair and placed in a corner of the room. He'd heard Katie's loud knock and identification and had hopped and scraped his way forward to get their attention. The steady thumping had likely come from Dane rocking the chair until one leg broke and he'd crashed onto his side.

"I've got backup on the way," Katie yelled from the front of the house.

"Dane's alive, but we need an ambulance," Royce yelled.

"On it!"

Royce gentled his voice. "Hey, buddy. You're going to be okay."

Dane had been stripped to his underwear, gagged, and left basically unattended. Scattered empty bottles of water and plates with partially eaten food littered the floor. Dane reeked of urine and feces, and his condition broke Royce's heart. He pulled a pair of latex gloves from his pocket and tugged them on before easing the gag from his mouth. Royce brushed a hand over Dane's filthy hair as the young man sobbed. Careful of where he stepped and touched, he worked Dane free from his bindings and eased him to a clean section of the floor. The young man immediately curled up into a protective ball.

Royce squatted beside him but didn't reach for him. He didn't know what Dane had endured and didn't want to make matters worse. Royce didn't see blood on Dane, but he'd noticed small burns on his abdomen that looked like Taser prong marks. The likely scenario played out in his mind like a movie. He imagined Dane looking up from his phone in the back seat of Cory's car and noticing they weren't going in the right direction. He might've spoken up, probably not alarmed yet, and Cory shot him with the Taser gun to disable him. That was probably the first time Dane soiled himself.

"An ambulance is on the way," Royce said. "I'll ride to the hospital with you, and I'll call your mom and Cayden when we get there. They've been so worried about you."

Dane's sobs eased, and he looked at Royce. "Thought I was going to die," he rasped.

"But you didn't. You're going to heal physically and emotionally." Blaring sirens announced the cavalry's arrival and helped Royce relax a little. "You have amazing people in your corner fighting for you. Remember that, okay?"

Doubt flooded Dane's expression, but he managed a curt nod.

EMTs arrived on the scene, and Royce got out of their way so they could assess Dane and get him ready for transport. Royce went outside and discarded his gloves into an evidence bag for the techs and waited in the fresh air until the EMTs brought Dane out. Royce gestured to Katie that he was riding with him, and she responded with a nod. Cory wasn't anywhere in sight, so he was either in the back of a squad car or already on his way to the precinct for booking. Royce tapped out a quick text to Sawyer and shared the good news about Dane. He asked him to notify Nina and Cade and bring them to the hospital. Royce received an immediate reply.

Sawyer: Thank God. I'm on it right now.

Dane's arrival at the hospital brought a rush of activity as the medical staff peppered him with questions as they assessed his condition and provided emergency care. Royce sat beside him, whispering words of encouragement when it seemed Dane wanted to shut down. The doctors needed to know what he'd been through to aid his recovery, and Royce wanted to prepare Dane for the next barrage of questions he would receive from Katie once he was stable. The evaluation seemed to take forever as the medical team moved around the bed, checking his vitals and inspecting his injuries, which were fairly minimal, all things considered.

The burn marks had come from getting hit by a Taser at close range. Royce learned there was a second set on his lower back, likely from Cory subduing Dane a second time to get him into the house. He'd sustained bruises from getting dragged and wrestled into the chair. Dane had defensive wounds on his hands from where he fought back, which was impressive after taking two hits from a Taser in quick succession. He'd injured his shoulder when he tipped his chair over, but they'd assess the extent of damage after seeing to his urgent needs. Cory hadn't sexually assaulted him, thank goodness, and had attempted to feed him and get him to drink water twice a day. Royce couldn't work up any gratitude that the little bastard had done the bare minimum to keep Dane alive. He'd let the guy soil himself for days and hadn't attempted to clean him. The indignity of what Dane endured made Royce see red.

Two nurses helped Dane shower in the attached bathroom once the initial assessment ended. He returned with their support, wearing a hospital gown and bright yellow grippy socks. He'd combed his wet hair out of his face, and Royce detected a whiff of mint toothpaste or mouthwash. The short walk back to the bed seemed to take it out of Dane, and he flopped against the raised mattress as if his legs had given up. Tackling his dehydration was the next task, and a male nurse named Kyle struggled to find a good vein to insert an IV needle. Dane lay there stoically, with barely a wince through the failed attempts, even though it probably hurt. Kyle asked the second nurse for assistance, and she retrieved a machine that scanned his arm to find a good vein for the IV. Royce was relieved enough for all of them once they'd achieved success and started the drip. And then it was just the two of them. The medical staff moved on to triage the next patient, leaving Dane to rest and allowing time for the IV fluids to do their thing.

Dane closed his eyes and looked peaceful for the first time since Royce rushed into Cory's house.

"Do you want to eat the graham crackers or drink the apple juice the nurses brought in for you?" Royce asked. They'd explained he needed to eat things that would be gentle on his stomach after doing without for several days, and the juice would help boost his blood sugar.

Dane shook his head, and tears leaked from under his closed eyelids. "I want to go home to my family."

"I asked my husband to tell your mom and Cayden that we found you. He would've brought them straight here."

Dry, chapped lips trembled. "Can I see them?"

"Let me see if they're here already." Royce pulled his phone from his pocket, but he didn't have any bars, and there was a satellite symbol where his Wi-Fi icon should've been. "I can't get reception in here. I'll check the waiting room."

Dane's hand snaked out and gripped his arm. His eyes snapped open, and wild blue eyes pleaded with him. "Don't leave."

"Okay. I'll just duck my head out and flag down a nurse," Royce said. "I'll stay where you can see me."

Dane released his arm. "Thank you."

Royce opened the door and poked his head outside just as the nurse named Kyle approached the room. They both jumped and shared an uneasy laugh. "Dane wants to know if his mom and brother are here yet."

"Yes, that's what I was coming to tell you," Kyle said. "They're in the waiting room and eager to see him. I wanted to double-check with Dane first before I brought them back."

"Please," Dane said hoarsely. "I need to see them."

Kyle nodded and turned around. Royce ducked back inside the room and reclaimed his spot beside the hospital bed. "I'll head out once they get here, but I'll be back to check on you."

"I'm not staying here any longer than I have to. I can rest and hy-drate at home," Dane said.

Royce couldn't blame the guy, but rushing out of there too soon might set his recovery back. "Only after they've checked your shoulder. I don't think you've dislocated it, but you could have a hairline fracture since all your weight came down on your shoulder."

"Fine," Dane conceded. "It does hurt like a son of a bitch."

"Do you want something for pain?" Kyle asked from the doorway.

"No," Dane replied. "I want a clear head when the police ask questions."

"Okay. Let me know if you change your mind." He stepped aside to let Dane's family enter.

Nina sat in a wheelchair, tears streaming down her face as Cayden pushed her to Dane's bedside. She rested her forehead on his thigh and sobbed, "My baby."

"Mama. I'm okay." Dane cried, too, as he carefully placed his hand on her head.

"You jackass," Cayden rasped. "You scared us to death." He came around to the other side of the bed, and Royce moved out of his way. Cay crashed into Dane's chest hard enough to make the air whoosh from his lungs.

A genuine smile cracked Dane's face. "Missed you too, Cay."

Royce caught Dane's attention and gestured that he was going to step out and give them privacy.

Dane nodded and mouthed, "Thank you."

Sawyer was still in the ER waiting room, but he wasn't alone.

Alec saw Royce first and rushed forward with a desperate expression on his face. "How is he?"

"They're still evaluating Dane's condition," Royce said, "but so far, the consensus is that he's dehydrated and a little banged up. They'll know more soon."

Sawyer hugged Royce tight, his relief a palpable thing. Families rarely got their loved ones back alive after an abduction, so they were incredibly lucky Cory hadn't killed Dane. Perhaps Katie's assumption was correct. Taking Dane was a spur-of-the-moment thing, but then he didn't know what to do with him. He trusted Katie would get to the bottom of it soon, and he wanted to be there when she did.

CHAPTER TEN

ALEC STOOD AT THE TWO-WAY MIRROR WITH RIGID POSTURE and his arms crossed over his chest. On the other side of the glass, Cory Sands sat alone in an interrogation room and seemingly returned his stare. "He can't see or hear us?" Alec asked.

"No," Sawyer said.

Alec had resisted Sawyer's suggestions to go home and rest now that Dane was safe. But his sense of responsibility wouldn't allow it, no matter what he or Royce said. Sawyer had assured Alec that Katie would leave Cory on ice for as long as necessary while she searched his house for every piece of evidence she could use to get a confession. He'd promised to call Alec in time so he could return to the precinct and observe the interrogation, but Alec had insisted on staying, choosing to catnap in the conference room where he worked. The fatigue had really done a number on Alec if he thought Cory possessed a super-natural skill that allowed him to see or hear through the glass.

But then Alec turned back to the mirror, and Cory's mouth curved into a deranged smirk. It had to be a coincidence, right? "Don't suppose you'd let me have a few minutes alone with him before Detective O'Connell gets here?" Alec asked.

"No," Sawyer repeated.

Royce leaned close and whispered, "He's growing on me."

Sawyer elbowed him and bit back a snort. Of course, Royce would like Alec when he wanted to go rogue. "He won't get away with what he's done."

"Should've never started this," Alec said. "I've psychoanalyzed every part of my personality to make sure I was nothing like Andrew." He lifted his arms and ran both hands through his hair. "I told myself a hundred times to forget about those trinkets before they consumed me. And who was I to think I could solve something the FBI couldn't?"

"More like wouldn't," Royce said.

Alec dropped his hands and shrugged. "Doesn't matter. I never should've come here. Dane and his family didn't deserve to get caught up in my bullshit."

"Wait a minute," Sawyer said, deciding it was time for some tough love. "If not for you, Monica Horton's family would never have known what really happened to her. You were the one who found the connection with the photographer and the red Camaro. You were the one who made the FBI stand up and take notice. That's no easy feat."

"It's hard as hell," Royce chimed in.

"And now, they're not only reviewing your evidence in Monica's case. They've invited you to sit at the big kids' table and have promised to help you match up the rest of the trinkets." Sawyer looked at Royce. "Has the FBI ever asked you to assist them?"

Royce shook his head adamantly. "Stonewalled me at every turn."

Alec's mouth twitched at the corners. "Are you guys playing good cop and better cop to cheer me up?"

"Nah," Royce said. "This is us being completely honest with you.

Maybe you got a little overzealous sometimes in your pursuit of justice, but your heart was in the right place. I can see that now."

"Thanks," Alec said. "I appreciate it."

The door to the interview room opened, and the trio turned their attention to the glass as Katie and a police officer sat down at the table. The smirk slid off Cory's face when he gave them his full attention. Katie noted the date and time and the participants in the room for the recording. She read Cory his rights again since a few hours had passed since his arrest. "Do you still wish to waive your right to counsel?"

"Yes." Cory raised a cuffed hand as high as he could and waggled his fingers in the air. "Hi, Alec."

"Mr. Bishop isn't in the room," Katie stated.

"Not in here," Cory said. "In there. Watching. Listening. Like I did with him and his whore. People who live in houses on a public beach shouldn't fuck in front of their wall of windows."

"Mr. Bishop isn't a member of the SPD, so he's nowhere near this interview room, Mr. Sands." Her tone was a warning to Cory and them. They'd broken several department rules by allowing Alec to observe, and it had better not bite them in the ass. "He's at the hospital enjoying a reunion with Dane Sutton. Looked like quite a love match."

Alec jerked his gaze to Sawyer, and he gestured for him to wait a minute. Katie had intended the comment to crack through Cory's placid demeanor, and her payout came immediately.

Cory's gaze darkened with rage, and his lips formed a cruel sneer. "That wasn't love. They rutted like filthy animals with no passion or genuine feeling between them. Just two men looking to get off."

Katie didn't physically react to her victory, though Sawyer suspected she mentally performed a happy dance. "So you admit to following Alec back home after he and Dane left the bar?"

Cory blinked as he realized his mistake. Instead of showing anger, he retreated into his cold, detached persona again. The Jekyll-and-Hyde shift was both fascinating and bone-chilling. Cory shrugged and said, "Yep. Parked down the street. But you already know this. If you'd gone back in the footage far enough, you probably would've seen me get out of the car and creep down to the beach for a front-row seat. Alec is even more gorgeous than I ever imagined." He shook his head slowly. "We could've been so good together. I would've shown him what passion really looks like."

Alec shuddered, and Sawyer rested a comforting hand on his shoulder.

"Thank you for telling me where to find additional evidence against you," Katie said. "Not that I need it after everything I found in your home and on your computer."

Cory chuckled. "And what did you find?"

"All the research you've done on Alec Bishop for the past fifteen months and the profile you made for him, detailing everything from his favorite foods to his preferred brand of shampoo." Katie cocked her head to the side. "How did you even find out about half of these things?"

"Interviews he's given since his book came out and posts he's made to his social media accounts," Cory said. "I found out about the shampoo when he posted a selfie in his bathroom. A portion of his shower was in the background, and I zoomed in." He cocked his head to the side, and Sawyer could tell he was thinking about saying more. Katie could sense it, too, and sat in silence instead of pressing on. "I know what brand of underwear he prefers, the side of the bed he sleeps in, and I know he likes his dildos thick and long."

Alec swayed but didn't go down. Royce moved to stand on his other side and also placed a supportive hand on his shoulder.

"How do you know those things?" Katie asked.

Cory sighed as if bored now. "Such an amateur question, Katie. Can I call you that?"

"You may not," she replied coolly. If Cory hoped to rattle her, he'd have to try harder.

"Detective O'Connell it is, then." Cory fidgeted slightly in the chair, so maybe he was more nervous than he'd wanted to let on. "I broke into his home, obviously. His book tour schedule was public, finding his address was a cinch, and his security is a joke." Cory cocked his head to the side. "I watched a video on how to pick a lock, bought a kit, and put my new skills into practice." He snapped his fingers to demonstrate how easy it had been.

"When did you go to his home?" Katie asked.

Cory rattled three dates, shocking everyone. "I had plenty of personal time saved up, and I listened to his audiobook during my road trips."

"Why did you keep breaking into his house?"

Cory tsked. "Detective, really. Maybe they should bring someone smarter in for this interview." He looked at the police officer next to Katie. "Tell the detective why I kept returning to my love's house." When the officer didn't respond, Cory looked him up and down. "Big, strong, silent type. Yum." He didn't get the reaction he'd hoped for there either, so he gave Katie his attention once more. "I wanted to feel closer to Alec. I learned something new about him from every visit and added the details to my profile, as you call it."

"Did you take anything?" Katie asked.

"I'm not a thief." Anger returned to Cory's honey-brown eyes, but he blinked it away. "But I left things behind."

Alec sucked in a sharp breath, and Sawyer worried he'd follow it up with a loud coughing fit and give them away. "Easy, short breaths, buddy."

"What kind of things?" Katie pressed.

Cory's sneer made Sawyer want to puke. "You can probably guess."

"I'd prefer you tell me."

He made a fist and crudely mimed jerking off. "In his shower, in his bed, while riding his big dildo, and on his couch. Little pieces of me everywhere. I wore his clothes, ate his food, read his books, and imagined what our lives could be like."

"And you stockpiled his favorite things in your home," Katie said. "Did you plan on kidnapping Mr. Bishop at some point?"

"No. I was going to make him love me as much as I love him. Knowing so much about him gave me a leg up." The lack of inflection in his voice made Cory's words even creepier. "But his whore came along and ruined it."

"You're referring to Dane Sutton as his whore?"

Cory's eyes turned nearly feral as he leaned toward Katie. "Did you know he sells himself for money? I didn't know that last week, but I learned it from Dane during our many conversations. He calls himself an escort, but we know what that really means. That's who Alec chose over me. Dane isn't good enough to share a meal with Alec, let alone his bed. I hate him."

"Dane?" Katie asked.

"Yes. I just couldn't find the courage to kill him."

"According to your browser history, you searched the least painful way to kill someone this morning. Is that why you'd gone home for lunch? Were you going to kill Dane?"

"Whore no more," he singsonged.

Royce and Sawyer exchanged stunned glances. They'd avoided a tragedy by the skin of their teeth.

Alec covered his mouth and staggered back from the glass. Was he going to be sick? Sawyer stepped into his line of sight to get his attention, and Alec gestured he was okay.

"So, that's a yes?" Katie pushed. "You had planned to kill Dane Sutton."

Cory cocked a brow. "Isn't that what I said?"

"No, you sang a little ditty," Katie told him. "And it was out of tune. For the record, and I need a simple yes or no here, did you plan to kill Dane Sutton?"

"Yes. Alec apologized for the shitty way he treated me. I needed to get Dane out of my way and clean his messes so I could bring Alec back to my house. I planned to fix him a nice dinner before teaching him what he really needed from a man."

"Fuck," Alec hissed. "I can't be in here."

Sawyer followed him out into the hallway to make sure he didn't push inside the interview room and attack Cody. He couldn't fault the urge, but he wouldn't condone the action. Luckily, Alec kept walking, muttering something under his breath Sawyer couldn't make out. They took the stairs down to the basement instead of the elevator, and Alec headed straight for the conference room, where he started to pack equipment.

"I won't be much longer," Alec said.

"No rush on my part. I'll be here a few more hours."

Alec snapped his head up. "No. I mean, yes, I'm leaving for the day. But I meant my stay in Savannah. I want to shoot some more background footage and wrap up a few things, but it shouldn't take more than a day. Two max."

"You don't need to rush out of here like the village elders are running you out of town," Sawyer teased, though he'd have led the charge barely forty-eight hours ago. "The FBI will make a confirmation on Monica's necklace, and I want you to be there when we call Talia with the news. The department will hold a press conference. Stay and be a part of that because it wouldn't have happened without your help."

Alec shook his head. "No, I need to take a different approach. I'm drawing too much attention to myself."

"Because of Cory Sands?"

"Don't tell me you wouldn't feel the same way." Alec shivered so hard he dropped a piece of equipment on the table. "Yeah, building the profiles of my likes and dislikes is creepy enough, but he broke into my house and did unspeakable things there." Alec trembled all over, then shook his head as if he could banish Cory's words from his head. "As awful as that is, I can't get past knowing he watched me have sex with Dane. Yeah, I should've considered someone could stroll on the beach in the middle of the night, but I was too consumed by Dane to care. And he was so wrong about the lack of passion and genuine emotion. I've had tons of meaningless hookups, and what I shared with Dane was special. I will not let Cory take that from me." He dropped into a chair and put his head in his hands. "I feel so violated. I can't possibly stay?"

"I think that feeling will follow you everywhere unless you tackle it head-on."

Alec slowly lifted his head. "What do you mean?"

"Have you ever sought treatment for your past trauma?"

Shaking his head, Alec said, "I chose action over reflection. I just don't see how talking about my problems will fix them. What can a therapist say to help me stop feeling like someone is watching me?"

"You won't know unless you try," Sawyer told him. "Don't let Cory take anything else from you."

Alec sighed heavily. "I'll consider it. I do really love it here." He met Sawyer's gaze. "And I want to make sure Dane is really okay before I go. He has a lot going on right now, but I'd like to be his friend if he'd let me." He smiled a little and added, "And maybe it could turn into something more later."

"You never know. I sure as hell never would've predicted marriage and fatherhood with Royce Locke."

Alec perked up. "Fatherhood?"

Oops. "I wasn't supposed to say anything yet." He'd given Royce a rough time for blurting out their secret, and there he went and did it with someone he hardly knew.

"I won't tell anyone," Alec promised.

Sawyer couldn't help imagining a role reversal of the punishment he'd given Royce. Oh, how he'd love to get on his knees for his husband. Sawyer believed Alec would keep his secret, so he aimed for a different tactic. "Hey, how do you feel about coming to our house for dinner tonight?"

CHAPTER ELEVEN

"ARE YOU SURE YOU DON'T MIND?" ROYCE ASKED. "WE DON'T want to intrude on this fine Wednesday evening."

Alec chuckled and stepped aside so their party of five could enter his spacious beach house. "You mean the way I blew into your life and wreaked all kinds of hell?"

Royce tilted his head and shrugged his shoulders. "I mean…"

Sawyer elbowed him hard. "Ignore him. My husband can be quite the brat."

"It's all good," Alec replied. "Hi, Kelsey."

"Hi, honey." She didn't bother asking how he was doing because the answer was evident in his wan complexion and the dark smudges under his eyes. But resilience and determination shimmered in Alec's green gaze. Hugging was Kelsey's love language, so she wrapped him up tightly before introducing Alec to her family. "This is my husband, Andrew," she said. "We're calling him Big Sexy for obvious reasons."

Alec's brow shot up as he scanned the tall, handsome man in front of him. Then his mouth quirked into a wry smile. "Because he has the same name as my serial killer father or because…"

Always a good sport, Big Sexy extended his hand and said, "All the above."

Alec winked at Kelsey. "Good on you." He met Ella next, who shyly buried her face in her father's neck. "Does anyone want a tour of the house before you start your beach photo shoot?"

"Me!" Kelsey said.

"Me! Me!" Ella chimed, her shyness all but forgotten as she clapped her adorable hands and matched her mama's energy.

"Where my girls go, I go too." Big Sexy gestured for Kelsey to lead the way.

When Sawyer moved to follow them, Royce snagged his wrist and held him in place. He leaned in close and pressed his lips to Sawyer's ear. "I'm not the only one with bratty behavior. I've yet to get even for that impromptu dinner party you hosted."

"One guest isn't a dinner party," Sawyer said. He turned and met his gaze, dark eyes dancing with mischief. "Not my fault you fell asleep before you could instruct me on how to be a good husband."

Royce cupped Sawyer's jaw and stroked his thumb over his lips. "You couldn't be a better husband if you tried." He pulled Sawyer in for a quick, hard kiss. "But I'll happily cheer on your efforts."

Sawyer laughed. "I just bet you will."

They kissed again, their mouths lingering long enough to make him wish for home, but they hadn't stopped by Alec's beach house for a casual hang. Kelsey and Sawyer had come up with an idea for a pregnancy announcement and Big Sexy, husband and father extraordinaire, moonlighted as an amateur photographer and had volunteered to snap the photographs.

"Oh! Oops!" The interruption came from a woman whose voice Royce didn't recognize.

He reluctantly pulled his lips away from Sawyer's and smiled at her. "Hello."

"Hi." She winked at Sawyer and said, "Damn, you did good."

Sawyer laughed. "Behave, Marina."

Ahhh. "You're Alec's producer." Holding out his hand, he said, "Royce Locke. It's nice to meet you."

Marina's cheeks went pink, and she extended the hand with a frosty margarita in it. "Oops again. I don't think we should let Ricky get near the blender anymore. Powerful stuff." She switched the drink to her other hand and shook Royce's. "It's nice to meet you too. Forgive my unprofessionalism."

"It's all good."

Sawyer nodded toward the drink. "I don't recall seeing margarita night on the production schedule."

Marina tipped her head back and laughed throatily. "Maybe not, but we damn well deserve it. What a week it's been so far." She gestured to Sawyer with her margarita and said, "He solved an almost thirty-year-old cold case. And you…" She took a sip of her drink as if she needed courage. "And you made a daring rescue."

"I wouldn't say it was daring," Royce hemmed.

"Dane's family would argue, and they'd be right." Marina raised her glass, saluting Sawyer and then Royce. "You're both amazing men. And now I need to go find some food to absorb the alcohol."

Ella's delighted squeals of joy caught their attention before Royce could swoop in and kiss Sawyer again. "Shen! Shen!"

"Ocean," Kelsey said, emphasizing the *O*, as she followed her excited daughter toward the wall of windows at the back of the house. "I see the perfect spot for our photographs. A nice clean stretch of sand without a ton of tourists."

"The lighting is perfect," Big Sexy said. "Let's get down to the beach because it won't last long. We might have thirty minutes." He'd insisted on taking the photos during the evening blue hour once Kelsey told him they'd be wearing white clothes for the pictures.

"Can I help with anything?" Alec asked.

"How good are you with writing in the sand? We need really crisp letters to stand out," Big Sexy said, suddenly sounding like a set designer.

"I'm your man," Alec said. He darted into the kitchen and returned with a long skewer used to roast marshmallows or hot dogs over an open fire. "This should make the letters look sharp and precise."

"You're hired." Big Sexy hoisted his camera bag onto his shoulders and handed a tote full of beach-and-baby-themed props to Alec.

The trio yielded to his detailed instructions, moving here, posing there, and having the best time of their lives. In most photos, Royce and Sawyer stood on either side of Kelsey and kissed her cheeks as she made heart hands over her belly or held up the sonogram. Big Sexy also took several photos of just the expectant dads with the sonogram. Alec had written Baby Locke Arriving February 2026 in the tidiest sand lettering Royce had ever seen. Ella let them borrow her sand bucket and shovel for some photos before she reclaimed them. Marina had traded the margarita for water and sat in the sand and watched Ella build a castle while they worked. Ricky filmed the entire photo shoot for them, and Royce looked forward to watching it on repeat until Lil Plum arrived.

When they parted ways in Alec's driveway, Royce hugged Kelsey longer than usual and rocked her gently. "You're our hero. We won't ever forget it, and Lil Plum will always know about the magnificent woman who gave her life."

Kelsey rested her cheek against his. "I love you guys so much, and I am so happy to be a part of your miracle."

"Damn it," Big Sexy said. "Here comes the waterworks."

Royce looked over as both Big Sexy and Sawyer wiped their eyes. Ella, tucked against her father's chest, clapped her hands. "I hope our Lil Plum is half as happy as Ella Jane."

Kelsey snorted as she stepped back. "Be careful what you wish for, honey. That little girl is a ray of sunshine, and she will burn you if you aren't careful."

Royce looked at his pretty princess in disbelief. "You say that all the time, but I've yet to see the proof."

"Go now!" Ella yelled before blowing kisses at Royce and Sawyer.

Kelsey gestured. "There's a tiny taste of her majesty's dominance. It's her world, and we just get to live in it."

"As it should be." Royce blew kisses back at her. "Love you, Ella Jane."

"I'll email a few photos after I've experimented with some edits," Big Sexy said as he placed Ella into her car seat.

"Don't edit too much," Sawyer said. "I want the photos to look like we do, not the supermodel versions of us."

He gave them a thumbs-up as he opened the passenger door for his wife. "Go now!" Big Sexy said, then dramatically imitated Ella's goodbye kisses.

Royce acted like he was grabbing them from the air while Sawyer blew some back. What a sight they must've made in the driveway. Kelsey's boisterous laughter in the front seat said it was comedy gold. They waved as Big Sexy's vehicle backed down the driveway.

"How long is the Big Sexy thing going to last?" Royce asked once they got into his SUV. "It evokes weird things."

"Well, calling him Andrew evokes weird things for me right now," Sawyer said. "Maybe we can come up with our own nickname for him."

"I can get on board with that," Royce said. "Something to do with his Scottish heritage."

"Fine," Sawyer said. "You're in charge of that. Do you want to grab something to eat while we're out or eat leftovers?"

Royce put the SUV in reverse and backed out of the driveway. "Leftovers." Three nights into their week, and they'd already had two pseudo dinner parties. "And then I want you naked and all to myself."

"You won't get any arguments from me."

Back at home, they changed out of their pristine white clothes in favor of loose shorts before removing the leftovers from the refrigerator and setting them out buffet-style on the kitchen island. They filled their plates, reheated whatever needed it, and tucked in. Royce devoured his portion of the eggplant Parmesan casserole and forked a bite from Sawyer's plate.

"I used to hate eating leftovers as an adult, no matter how good the meal," Royce said. "It reminded me of how broke we were as kids, eating the same thing for three or four days in a row."

"And now?" Sawyer asked, moving his plate closer to Royce so he could steal another bite of the casserole.

"I changed my thinking after attending the Sawyer Locke School of Gratitude and Mindfulness." Royce basked in the warmth he experienced every time he attached his last name to Sawyer's first. It made him downright giddy. His husband's smirk let Royce know his detour to Happy Town hadn't gone unnoticed. "Instead of seeing the leftovers as punishment or embarrassment, I look back in awe at the way my mom held everything together when it would've been so much easier to give up. Even when she was as sick as Nina, she fought hard until the end. Being wasteful feels like a disservice to her memory." He snagged another bite from Sawyer's plate and lifted his fork in the air. "To you, Mama."

Sawyer saluted her too.

"Did you save room for dessert?" Royce asked. "I haven't eaten all the chocolate mousse yet." Though it had been a close call after he found Oreos stashed in the pantry. Hell, he'd hidden them so well that he'd forgotten about them. Crumbled cookies would be perfect to mix into the mousse.

"Get the Oreos," Sawyer said as he retrieved the whipped dessert from the refrigerator.

Royce didn't bother asking how he knew about the discovery. He probably told on himself when he slept. Or…Sawyer had stumbled upon the stash and hit it a few times. Or…it was Sawyer's stash all along. Maybe Royce hadn't forgotten about it because he hadn't hidden the cookies there. He studied his husband's expression and realized it was too innocent.

Dolly ran into the kitchen, working her toy over like she got paid per squeak. Royce looked down to see which of her plushies she'd tormented them with and saw a fuzzy pink purse he hadn't bought for her. He looked at Sawyer, whose innocent expression turned into a guilty smile before his eyes.

"When did you have time to buy that?" Royce asked.

"Um, yeah, I forgot to tell you something during all the excitement yesterday."

"I'm listening now," Royce said cautiously.

"Remember how I told you not to hang the sonogram on the refrigerator until after the reveal, but you did it anyway?"

Royce chuckled and shook his head. "This isn't how confessions go, Asshole. And what does that have to do with Dolly's toy? Did you steal it or something?"

"Evangeline swung by yesterday to spoil Dolly and Bones with new treats and toys," Sawyer said.

"Oh no." Royce knew exactly where this was going.

"Yep. She saw the sonogram on the refrigerator and called me at work. She was very upset that we hadn't told her."

"This is on me," Royce said. "I'm sorry."

"Oh, good," Sawyer sighed, placing a hand over his heart. "So glad you agree."

Royce narrowed his eyes, sensing a trap. "Agree about what?"

"That this is your fault, which is exactly what I told my mother," Sawyer said, bolting to the left to avoid Royce's reach.

Countering his move, Royce ended up on the opposite side of the kitchen island, where he could stare his husband down. "You said what?"

"I told her *I* wanted to tell you right away but that *you* insisted that Evangeline O'Neal wait to get the news like everyone else."

"Excuse me?" Royce knew that was complete bullshit, but he played along, feigning his outrage. Forget the chocolate mousse. Royce was about to have some delicious fun with his husband, and it would be dairy-, fat-, and carb-free. Sawyer's chest rose and fell, his excitement turning his dark eyes into shimmering black diamonds. Stalking around the island, Royce kept Sawyer in his sights as he tried to predict which way he would go.

"And then I confessed that you told Eddie about Lil Plum first."

Sawyer cut and run before he even finished the sentence, and Royce was in hot pursuit. It had been a few months since they'd played this game. Royce had taken him down to the rug and mounted him the last time. But he'd let the fun play out and chase his prey a little longer. Sawyer misjudged his speed taking a turn into the hallway and nearly clipped his shoulder against the wall. Royce's growing erection should've made it harder for him to run, but it only made him pump his legs faster. Sawyer did crash into the doorjamb as he cut a hard turn into their bedroom, but it had nothing to do with clumsiness and everything to do with the enormous gray cat hauling ass to escape their room before they fucked like animals.

Royce leaped over the fleeing feline and sprinted through the door, sensing his prey was near. Nostrils flared as he spotted the rounded, muscular ass he was about to plow. He lunged forward, crashing into his husband's back and tackling him to the mattress.

"Did you hurt anything precious when you crashed into the door?" Royce asked.

Sawyer bucked under him, pushing that sweet ass against his erection. "See for yourself."

Royce reached around him and slid a hand under Sawyer's pelvis, stroking the perfect hard-on he discovered there. "Oh yeah. You're in fucking form."

"It's all talk until you prove it," Sawyer taunted.

And so Royce did, dragging Sawyer's shorts down before removing his own and then using his bodyweight to keep his husband pinned while reaching for the lube. A *snick* from the cap, a drizzle of cool liquid over Sawyer's puckered entrance, and Royce slid a finger all the way inside him. Sawyer groaned and pushed his ass against Royce's hand, urging him to do more. A quick nip on Sawyer's neck reminded him he wasn't in charge, which only seemed to make him wilder.

"I won't go easy," Royce warned.

"Who asked you to?"

"And I won't be fast."

"Thank fuck," Sawyer said. "It would be a big letdown if I only got a few pumps after you chased me down and threw me to the bed."

"So feisty," Royce said as he plunged two fingers into Sawyer's tight channel, working his hole just the way they both liked. Slower, faster, harder, and gentler. Changing the tempo and intensity until his man's entire existence was focused on the nerve endings in that tight little pucker and the happy button Royce kept pegging. "Give me your dick."

"Ask nicely," Royce said.

Sawyer writhed and humped the mattress, looking for the friction to make him come. "Dick now."

Royce bit his lip to keep from laughing at Sawyer's desperation. He eased his fingers from his ass, and Sawyer watched over his shoulder as Royce slicked himself with lube. Instead of pushing straight in, Royce rubbed the head of his dick around the rim of his sensitive opening.

"Shove that cock inside me and make me come."

Royce slowly pushed in, watching the first few inches sink inside him. It took all his willpower not to bury himself deep and rut inside Sawyer until they both found release. But that would be too easy, and their sensual game would be over too soon. Royce eased back and pushed in, keeping his thrusts frustratingly shallow.

Sawyer bucked under him, trying to get more of Royce's dick. "You won this round. Now, fuck me properly."

Royce nuzzled against Sawyer's neck. "Not sure you can use fuck and proper in the same sentence."

Sawyer released a savage growl and used the power of his legs to drive them both backward, off the bed, and landing in the fancy velvet chair he insisted on putting in the bedroom. When Royce's ass landed on the soft fabric, he understood the merit of having the chair in the room, especially when Sawyer rode his dick reverse-cowboy style. The beauty and magnificence of Sawyer, and the play of muscles as he used Royce's body to pleasure himself, stole his breath. He spread Sawyer's cheeks, watching that glorious ass work his cock, gripping him tighter as his climax drew nearer. Sawyer bounced harder and faster, his thighs slapping against Royce's. His breathing changed, coming quicker and choppier. And then he stilled, moaning Royce's name as his channel clamped around Royce's dick as he climaxed.

Royce grabbed Sawyer's hips and thrust into him, needing more friction to get off. Sawyer's body went pliant, heavy and sated against him, making it hard for Royce to get any leverage to move. He detected a snort and knew what his husband was up to. "Ride my cock."

"Can't feel my legs," Sawyer protested, adding a yawn and somehow making his body heavier. "You let all the air out of my muscles."

Royce dug his fingertips into the ticklish spot in Sawyer's ribs, and he bolted upright. Using that momentum, Royce demonstrated his strength by taking Sawyer to the rug on his hands and knees. He wrapped an arm around Sawyer's upper chest to hold him in place and fucked him to orgasm. They collapsed onto the carpet and stared up at the ceiling, panting to catch their breath.

"This is going to hurt tomorrow," Sawyer whispered.

"Tomorrow?" Royce asked. "My postcoital glow hasn't even left yet, and I'm already aware of rug burn on my knees and a throbbing in my hamstring."

"I might've broken a toe when I tripped over the cat."

"Poor Bones," Royce said.

"Poor Bones?" Sawyer lifted his foot to show that his big toe had turned an ugly shade of purple. "I'll be lucky if I can walk tomorrow."

"Eh, it will make it easier for me to catch you so my hammy can heal."

Sawyer's glower turned into a grin as they laughed about their ridiculousness. "We'll likely have to dial things back a bit when Lil Plum arrives."

Royce chuckled. "Or at least save the rowdiest stuff for when she goes to Evangeline's house." He pinned Sawyer with a dark look. "If she ever talks to us again."

Sawyer waved him off. "She's deliriously happy for us and understood why we wanted to wait to make one big announcement."

"Two if you consider the one we need to make at work," Royce said. "I have an idea."

"I'm afraid to ask, but…what is it?"

Royce rolled over onto his side and propped his head up on his elbow, ignoring the twinge in the back of his thigh. "A mock crime scene." When Sawyer scowled, Royce held up a hand. "Hear me out. Nothing gross. But there are clues they need to find to figure out what we're trying to announce."

"You want us to play a live version of Clue in the precinct?"

"I was thinking more like a scavenger hunt, and the items will reveal our special news," Royce said. "But your idea isn't bad."

"Wait. That wasn't my idea. I was trying to get clarity on yours."

"No, no," Royce said. "I'm not a glory hound who needs to steal someone's credit. Let's run with yours."

"Ro, we're going to order dozens of sugar cookies that are shaped like onesies. We'll have the baker write a cutesy message in icing, and we'll pass them out."

"That's kind of tame," Royce said. "Where's the pizazz?"

Sawyer lifted his leg and showed off his gross toe. "Your idea of pizazz gets us in trouble sometimes."

Royce's hamstring spasmed as if to prove Sawyer's point, which he conceded with a sigh.

"And my idea includes eating sugar cookies. No one is eating cake or cookies that came from a fake crime scene. Besides, our sweet Lil Plum isn't a crime."

"No, she's our precious miracle," Royce said. "You're always so smart."

198

"Married you, didn't I?" Then Sawyer grimaced. "Ow. It's throbbing."

"Again? Damn, I'm good, but not that good."

"My toe, Dickhead," Sawyer said.

"Here, let me help you up. We might need to get that checked out." Royce tried to roll to his knee, but his hamstring spasmed, and he landed back down on the rug, holding the back of his aching leg.

Sawyer's body shook with laughter. "We're too young for those necklaces that alert emergency services when we fall."

"Damn thing would get the paramedics here every time we had sex," Royce said.

They shared a laugh for a few more minutes before they joined forces to get off the floor. They limped into the kitchen to retrieve ice for their injuries and eat dessert. Royce grabbed the Oreos and the bowl of chocolate mousse, and Sawyer grabbed the ice packs.

"Good call on the chair, by the way," Royce said, then winced on his next step.

"I can tell."

"So worth it."

CHAPTER TWELVE

E VANGELINE CURLED HER ARM AROUND SAWYER'S WAIST. "I love
you so much."

Sawyer draped an arm over her shoulders and rested his temple on top of her head. "I love you too. But I'm still not ready to make
the announcement."

His mother released an exasperated sigh. "Fine, but it's getting
late, and people will start leaving soon."

"Not the ones that matter, Mom." Sawyer didn't care if friends of
friends found out about their big news secondhand.

Everyone who mattered would be there, including some last-min-
ute guests Sawyer invited. He glanced over to where Royce gathered
with the Suttons, Jason, and Alec. Dane's physical injuries were on the
mend, but it would take longer for his emotional wounds to heal. Alec
had worried Dane would blame him for what happened and had braced
himself for rejection, but Sawyer witnessed the genuine smiles Dane
sent Alec's way, even if he'd chosen to sit across from him instead of
taking the empty chair next to Alec. With time and healing, Sawyer
thought they might have a chance at something special.

Nina sat with her face toward the sun and her eyes closed, a serene smile gracing her face. Sawyer was all too familiar with that expression because Vic had worn a similar one toward the end of his life. She'd made peace with the fact that this would be her final Labor Day celebration and was enjoying every second. She must've sensed his gaze on her because she opened her eyes and turned them in his direction. Her smile grew bigger, and she winked. Royce leaned forward to break their eye contact and pretended to scold her for flirting with his man. Sawyer couldn't hear the words they exchanged, but he recognized the gesticulation and gleam in his gray eyes. Nina swatted Royce out of the way to clear her line of sight. Sawyer winked back, and she waggled her fingers.

Flirting hadn't been the intention behind Nina's wink. The gesture was pure gratitude after the conversation they'd had two weeks ago when he'd taken her to the hospital to see Dane after his rescue. She'd been an emotional wreck, relieved and full of gratitude that Dane had survived, but terrified about what the future might hold for her sons. Sawyer had simply reached for her hand and told Nina that he and Royce would always look out for them. They'd always have a place to go for the holidays, an ear to bend, a shoulder to lean on, and people in their corner cheering them on. Her tears had turned to relief then, and she radiated peaceful acceptance now.

Sawyer spotted his father heading inside the house and excused himself to go talk to him. There were some things he wanted to tell his dad before they made the big announcement. Barron had always been the midnight backdrop to Evangeline's diamond bright star, and he'd never complained. His dad seemed more than happy to bask in her brilliance, but sometimes quiet personalities like his got overlooked. Credit went to other people when it should be shared or even given to others. Sawyer, a proud mama's boy since birth, loved his father dearly but worried he didn't always give Barron the recognition he deserved. That truth became even more apparent as he watched Royce and Eddie stumble their way through a reconciliation.

"Hey, Dad," he called out.

Barron jerked his head out of the refrigerator with a partially eaten cupcake in his hand. He swallowed the bite and held up the treat with a victorious smile. "Why didn't anyone tell me we had cupcakes?"

Sawyer bit back a laugh. "Because those go with the big announcement Royce and I are about to make."

"Oops." Then the words clicked. He looked into the refrigerator and noticed the candy baby bottles and rattles decorating the tops of the cupcakes. "You're having a baby!"

"We are," Sawyer confirmed. "Kelsey is the biological mother and our surrogate."

Barron pulled Sawyer into a fierce hug, his happiness bubbling out of him in joyous laughter. When he stepped back from the embrace, he looked around the house. "You didn't tell me before your mother, did you? I can't live with that."

Sawyer laughed. "She knows. I hadn't planned to tell her, but she stumbled onto the news when she popped by to spoil the pets while we were at work."

Barron grimaced and looked from his hand to the rest of the cupcakes. "I don't know what to do now."

"Eat the evidence," Sawyer said.

His dad devoured the rest of it in two bites. "Done. Wow. This is the absolute best news. I am so happy for you."

"Thank you." Sawyer pulled back from the hug. "That's why I followed you inside. I wanted to say how much I appreciate the example you've set for me. People have always said I'd make a wonderful father, and I know that's because of you."

Tears filled Barron's eyes. "Thank you, Sawyer. I appreciate your generous words, but you made fatherhood so easy." He nodded toward the lawn, where Sawyer's brother and sister engaged in competitive lawn games. "I can't always say that about your siblings."

They shared a laugh, which drew Evangeline's attention on the patio. She came inside and joined them, wrapping her arms around Barron's waist and leaning her head against his shoulder. "Did Sawyer tell you the good news?"

"Only after he caught me eating one of the baby announcement cupcakes."

Evangeline sighed and shook her head. "I knew I should've hidden them in the garage refrigerator."

"Is everything ready to go with the outdoor TV?" Sawyer asked.

"Yes. Andrew, the sweet dear, emailed the video with a montage of photos set to music," Evangeline replied.

"How many times have you watched it?" Barron asked.

"Too many to count. I'll happily cue the video when you're ready." Evangeline reached for Sawyer's hand. "Are you ready?"

"I am. Let's collect my husband."

Royce must've read Sawyer's intention because he stood up and crossed the lawn without a single gesture. "Are we ready?"

"Yes." Sawyer kissed Royce's cheek, and then they both gestured for Kelsey. She stood between them as she had during the photos, looking more radiant than one person had a right to. "Family, friends," Sawyer said loudly. Most people turned toward them, but a few stragglers continued talking, including his siblings, who were arguing over cornhole scoring.

Eddie whistled loudly, and the gathering got so quiet you could've heard a feather land in the lush grass. "My sons are trying to make an announcement," he said.

Royce snorted, but Sawyer knew the gesture meant a lot to him.

"Thanks, Eddie," Sawyer said. "Royce, Kelsey, and I—" Loud music boomed from the patio speakers and drowned out what he was about to say.

"Oops," Evangeline said. "I got trigger-happy in all my excitement." She fiddled with the remote. The volume went up and down. The video rewound, fast-forwarded, and rewound again.

Several gasps echoed in the crowd as their friends and family got the gist of the announcement before they could make it. They leaped from the chairs and swarmed the patio, showering them with love, hugs, and congratulations. Sawyer met his mom's remorseful gaze and mouthed, "Thank you." He'd rehearsed what he wanted to say, but it always came out stilted. Her mistake worked out much better for him.

"We have cupcakes to celebrate," Evangeline announced.

"I'll go get them while you figure out how to restart the video from the beginning," Barron said.

Luckily, Big Sexy swooped in and fixed it right up. Everyone gathered around with cupcakes in hand to watch the slideshow of beautiful photos as "I Can't Wait to Love You" by Niko Moon played. Leaning his head against Royce's, Sawyer got swept away by the beautiful lyrics, the memories of the promises they'd made to each other, and all the precious milestones awaiting them. Sawyer looked at his husband, best friend, and father of their child. "I could not ask for more."

"And you'll never have to."

EPILOGUE

LUCY, NOW ROCKING A LIME-GREEN AND VIOLET PIXIE, MOVED the transducer over Kelsey's belly during their twenty-week scan. Beside him, Sawyer squeezed his hand hard enough to break his fingers.

"Is our Lil Sweet Potato cooperating?" Royce asked.

"Mm-hmm," Lucy said. "Sure is. Do you want to find out the—?"

"Yes!" Sawyer and Kelsey blurted before she could finish.

Lucy laughed and looked at Royce. "And you too?"

"We already know, but I would like to confirm it," he said.

"Do you still think you're having a girl?" Lucy asked.

"A girl," the trio said.

"Hmmm." Her response gave nothing away, and the twinkle in her eyes said it was no accident.

"Hmmm?" Sawyer asked. "Or mm-hmmm?"

Lucy made eye contact with them, one after the other, and then a huge smile spread across her face. "It's a girl!"

The three of them cheered loudly. Kelsey could only manage an air pump with her fists at the moment, and Sawyer shimmied in his chair. Royce pressed a hand over his chest so his heart couldn't beat its way out.

"This is the best birthday present ever," he told Sawyer and Kelsey.

"You're welcome," Kels said.

Sawyer slapped Royce's leg repeatedly. "This is so amazing."

"You're still going to use fruits as her nickname though, aren't you?" Royce teased.

"You haven't picked out a name yet?" Lucy asked.

"We have," Royce said casually.

"I only know her middle name," Sawyer said. "It's Grace."

"Very Southern," Lucy said. "But why don't you know your daughter's first name?"

"Because Royce would have to tell me his Aunt Tipsy's legal name since we're naming our daughter after her," Sawyer said. "It's a game we've been playing for years. I've been guessing, but I never get it right."

"Any person with a smartphone could learn that information," Kelsey teased. "You're a police officer who's trained to find people."

"True," Sawyer agreed. "But where's the fun in that?"

Lucy's eyebrow shot up. "When do you plan to find out?"

"Probably when we're filling out the paperwork for her birth certificate, if my guesses don't improve."

"He's gotten so close," Royce said.

"Oh my goodness!" Kelsey exclaimed, looking from her cell phone to Royce. "That's the cutest name ever. And the most Southern of Southern names."

"Hey!" Sawyer whined. "No fair."

He'd been the best sport about...well, everything, and Royce took pity on him. "Can I have a sonogram, Lucy?"

"Sure."

She handed him a black-and-white photo, which he extended to Sawyer. "Meet your daughter, Darla Grace."

To be continued...

Brokered Betrayals on December 16, 2025. You can preorder now here: mybook.to/Brokered_Betrayals

Staying in touch is easier than ever and prettier too! Would you like to follow me on all the socials, signup for my newsletter, or join my Facebook reader's group? You can do all those things by checking out this handy hub on my website @ www.aimeenicolewalker.com/links

OTHER BOOKS BY
AIMEE NICOLE WALKER

Curl Up and Dye Mysteries
Dyeing to be Loved
Something to Dye For
Dyed and Gone to Heaven
I Do, or Dye Trying
A Dye Hard Holiday
Ride or Dye
Curl Up and Dye Box Set

Road to Blissville Series
Unscripted Love
Someone to Call My Own
Nobody's Prince Charming
This Time Around
Smoke in the Mirror
Inside Out
Prescription for Love

Welcome to Blissville Collection (Both M/M Blissville series)
Volume One
Volume Two

The Lady is Mine Series
The Lady is a Thief
The Lady Stole My Heart

Queen City Rogue Series
Broken Halos
Wicked Games
Beautiful Trauma

Zero Hour Series

Ground Zero
Devil's Hour
Zero Divergence
Zero Hour Box Set

Sawyer and Royce: Matrimony and Mayhem
The Magnolia Murders
Marriage is Murder
Killer Honeymoon

Sawyer and Royce: Felonies and Fatherhood
The Paternity Puzzle

Sinister in Savannah Series
Ride the Lightning
Mr. Perfect
Pretty Poison
Sinister in Savannah Box Set

Savannah Universe Standalone Books
Invisible Strings
Bad at Love
About Last Night
Just Say When
Single in Savannah Box Set

Standalone Novels
Second Wind

Fated Hearts Series
Chasing Mr. Wright
Rhythm of Us
Surrender Your Heart
Perfect Fit

Redemption Ridge Series
Guys Like Him
The Fortunate Son
Saints Like Him
Friends Like Them
The Keeper
The Beautiful Mess
Starts With a Bang

Coauthored with Nicholas Bella
Undisputed
Circle of Darkness (Genesis Circle, Book 1)
Circle of Trust (Genesis Circle, Book 2)

ACKNOWLEDGMENTS

Many, many thanks to Charity, Sandra, and Lori for your editing services and for keeping me in line. These ladies are consummate professionals and are pure joy to work with. And much love to Natasha Snow for this gorgeous cover and to Stacey Ryan Blake for her stunning interior designs. All of you make my books sparkle and shine so beautifully—inside and out. I thank my lucky stars that I get to work with such wonderfully talented people.

Sending much love to Melinda James Rueter and Racheal Yunk for bravely reading my rough drafts and providing priceless feedback. And I don't know where I'd be without CC Belle, my amazing personal assistant, who brings organization and so much joy into my life. Love you, ladies!

xoxo

Aimee

ABOUT
AIMEE NICOLE WALKER

Aimee Nicole Walker is an international bestselling author of Male/ Male contemporary romance and romantic suspense novels. Her stories guarantee hunks with big…hearts, lots of humor and heat, and the occasional homicide. Aimee is a lifelong dreamer, an avid reader, and an off-key singer. Only two of those traits help her craft captivating characters and charming communities where everyone is welcome. She uses the other quirk to entertain her pets during writing breaks.

Aimee has loved the same guy for over thirty years. Her husband is the reason she can write romance novels, and he's possibly inspired a fictional murder plot a time or ten. They share three adult children, two adorable grandsons, and a menagerie of pets that don't include goats or donkeys…yet. Love inspires everything she does, books keep her sane, and coffee is the magic elixir that fuels her day.

Let's stay in touch!

Would you like to learn more about my work, sign up for my newsletter, or follow my social media accounts? Here's your fast pass to all things Aimee: